Emergency!

"That's funny. The door isn't locked," Ned said as he swung it open. "Mom's usually a fanatic about that." He raised his voice and called, "Mom?"

No one answered. "Mom?" he called again, striding into the kitchen. "You home?"

Still no answer. "Maybe she just ran out for a second," I suggested.

"Could be," Ned said. "I'm going to quickly check upstairs. Maybe she's resting or something."

I followed him up the stairs. Together we peered into the master bedroom. It was quiet and empty, the setting sun turning the white carpet orange.

Ned shrugged. "I guess she must have gone out and forgotten to lock up," he said. "I'm just going to dump my stuff in my room."

He opened the door to his room, which was at the other end of the hallway. Then I heard him gasp. "No!"

My heart thudded. I ran down the hall and peered over his shoulder as he stood frozen in the doorway. My mouth fell open in shock.

There on Ned's bedroom floor lay his mother. Her eyes were closed, her face white. And she wasn't moving.

NANCY DREW
girl detective®

Available from Aladdin Paperbacks

NANCY DREW

girl detective ®

#26

Fishing for Clues

CAROLYN KEENE

Aladdin Paperbacks

New York   London   Toronto   Sydney

♠ALADDIN PAPERBACKS
An imprint of Simon & Schuster Children's Publishing Division
1230 Avenue of the Americas, New York, NY 10020
Copyright © 2007 by Simon & Schuster, Inc.
All rights reserved, including the right of
reproduction in whole or in part in any form.
NANCY DREW, NANCY DREW: GIRL DETECTIVE, ALADDIN PAPER-
BACKS, and related logo are registered trademarks of Simon & Schuster, Inc.
Manufactured in the United States of America
First Aladdin Paperbacks edition October 2007
10 9 8 7 6 5 4 3 2 1
Library of Congress Control Number 2007921469
ISBN-13: 978-1-4169-3525-4
ISBN-10: 1-4169-3525-8

Contents

A Running Start

N ancy, I have bad news." My friend Bess Marvin's blue eyes were sorrowful as she gazed at me. "It's about George."

"What? What's wrong with George?" I asked, my heart skipping a beat. "Is she hurt?"

"Not exactly," Bess replied. "It's just that she has completely LOST HER MIND!" She said the last words in a shout.

"Who's lost her mind?" My other best friend, Bess's cousin George Fayne, opened the door of Bess's bedroom and stepped inside.

"You, apparently." I looked George up and down. "Although I have to say, I'm having a hard time seeing it." She was wearing low-cut black workout pants and a gray hoodie, and her short, tousled dark hair was pulled back in a headband, which was a pretty standard look for her.

"What did I do?" George asked Bess, her forehead wrinkling.

"Oh, nothing," Bess said. "Only signed all three of us up to run in a marathon, that's all!"

"Excuse me?" I choked on the sip of iced tea I'd just taken. "Did you say *marathon*?"

"It's not a marathon," George protested. "It's just a ten-K run for charity. Piece of cake—my grandmother could do it."

"Wasn't your grandmother in the Olympics?" I murmured. I knew that wasn't true, but it is true that athletic ability runs in George's family. She's a natural. Her energy level is so high that I've actually seen her dance in place while waiting to cross the street. She can eat whatever she wants and never gain an ounce, unlike the rest of us mortals. She's also a techno-geek, but that's another story.

"It'll be fun!" George was insisting. "It's in a month, so we've got plenty of time to train. And I've got a great routine already worked out."

I could see the gleam in her brown eyes. It worried me. I mean, I'm not *un*athletic—I like a tennis match or a pickup soccer game as much as the next girl—but George can be kind of a fanatic. I had visions of her counting off like a drill sergeant as Bess and I did hundreds of crunches and push-ups.

"I don't know," I started to say. "I've got a lot going on right now. . . ."

"Like what?" George said. "You haven't had a new case in weeks. Face it, Nan, you've caught every criminal in River Heights. There just aren't any left."

I had to laugh. See, I'm a detective. And even though I'm not a pro, in a place like River Heights, I usually manage to find plenty of mysteries to keep me busy. You'd be amazed how many people need help—locating a long-lost relative, finding out who's been trampling their vegetable patch, stuff like that. But the truth was, my life had been pretty uneventful lately.

"I guess I could fit it in," I said. "After all, it is for charity."

"Nancy Drew!" Bess cried. "You're supposed to be on my side!" She flopped dramatically back on her bed. "What about charity toward me?" She sat up again. "Have mercy on me, you two. I do *not* run. I'm not built for it!"

George and I both looked at her. Bess's blue eyes are paired with long, soft blond hair and dimples. She is slightly shorter and curvier than either George or me, but she definitely isn't fat. In fact, Bess is totally gorgeous. Boys have been known to stare after her so long that they walk into walls.

"I don't know what you're talking about," George said. "You've got legs, don't you? That's all you need."

"Well, I'm not doing it," Bess snapped. "I read in a magazine that running is terrible for you."

"It's for a good cause," I said. "Um, by the way, George, what cause is it?"

"Environmental Action," George said. "You don't get a better cause than that."

"No way," Bess said, and folded her arms.

George sighed. "Oh, well, I guess Deirdre's team will get all the glory, then."

"What?" Bess cried. Deirdre Shannon is one of her least favorite people. None of us are all that fond of her, in fact. But Bess feels especially strongly about her, ever since the time Deirdre "accidentally" snagged her heel in Bess's gown and ripped off half the skirt because Bess went to a benefit dance with a boy Deirdre liked.

"Yeah," George said now. "The team that raises the most money gets a feature in the *River Heights Bugle*. And Richard Solomon has pledged that whichever team comes in first, he'll match however much money they've managed to raise on their own."

"Wow!" I said. "That's generous." Richard Solomon is a local businessman who is running for governor. My boyfriend, Ned Nickerson, is volunteering on his campaign.

"Who's on Deirdre's team?" Bess asked.

"Tom Foley, for one," George answered.

I raised my eyebrows. Tom Foley is our town's track star. He is also the boy with whom Bess had gone to the benefit dance.

Bess's eyes narrowed. "Are you serious? She must be paying him."

"Could be," George said. "All I know is, I saw Deirdre this morning when I was signing our team up, and she saw your name on the list and laughed."

Bess gasped in outrage. "She did? That little—well, that settles it. Fine." She took a deep breath. "I'm in, and I'm in to win!"

I had to turn away to hide my smile. I was almost positive George had just made up the whole Deirdre thing, but whatever. It worked.

As I turned back I caught sight of Bess's alarm clock. Oh, no! "Five o'clock already?" I moaned. "I'm supposed to be meeting Ned for coffee right this minute! I've got to go!"

"Tomorrow morning at six a.m.," George called after me as I hurried off. "Bess and I will pick you up at your house. Wear running clothes."

"Six a.m.? That's the crack of dawn!" I heard Bess squawk.

As I ran down the sidewalk to my car I flipped open my cell phone with one hand and dug in my bag for my keys with the other. I hit Ned's speed-dial number. He picked up just as I opened my car door—and my alarm went off. "Ack!" I yelped, and stabbed at the Disarm button. "Stupid thing!"

"I'm going to assume you're not talking to me," Ned replied, laughing. "Hi, Nancy."

"I'm sorry, Ned," I said breathlessly. "I'm—"

"On your way," he finished for me. "I know, I know. Don't worry about it. Just drive safe and I'll see you in ten minutes."

I smiled into the phone. "You're the best. See you in ten."

Ten minutes later I pulled into a parking space across from Mugged, Ned's and my favorite coffee hangout, and hurried inside.

He was sitting at our usual spot in the window, peering at the screen of his laptop, looking adorable as always. Two mocha lattes steamed on the table. He knows what I like. I slid into the seat opposite him and gave him a quick hello peck on the lips. "Sorry I'm late."

The corners of his brown eyes crinkled as he smiled at me. "You haven't been late in a while. Does this mean you have a new case?"

"No, just a new cause." I told him about the 10-K run and how George had gotten Bess to agree to do it by playing on her dislike for Deirdre Shannon.

"I'm a little worried about how psyched George is," I added. "She wants us to go running at six tomorrow morning. Ugh! That's brutal."

"Six? That's nothing," Ned scoffed. "My dad's been on this manly activity kick lately and he dragged me out to the river at *five* yesterday morning to go fishing. The sun wasn't even up yet when we got there."

"Ouch," I said, wincing. "On a Sunday, too! Isn't it supposed to be a day of rest?"

He grinned. "Actually, it turned out to be a lot of fun. We rented one of those little putt-putt motorboats from the marina next to the golf course. You know Dad—he always has to do it right, so he had on his special fishing hat with all the fly-fishing lures in it, none of which he's ever used in his life. So then we sat there for like half an hour and he kept going on about how this was the way life should be, just men and nature, and planning out this whole series of articles about it for the newspaper." Ned's dad is the publisher of the *River Heights Bugle*. "And nothing was biting at all, and I was getting hungrier and hungrier because he wouldn't let us stop for breakfast, and then all of a sudden his line started wiggling."

"What was it?" I asked, skimming cinnamon-dusted foam off my latte.

"I figured it would be a log or an old boot or something, but it turned out to be this monster catfish,"

Ned said. "It must have weighed twenty pounds. And Dad reeled it in just like a pro. I was impressed. For a minute, anyway." His grin got wider.

"Uh-oh," I said. "What happened?"

Ned turned his laptop so that I could see the screen. "One picture is worth a thousand words," he said. "Or, in this case, two pictures."

I peered at the image. In the background was the early-morning river, steam still rising in wisps off its surface, and the rolling green of the golf course. In the foreground was James Nickerson, Ned's father, standing up in the boat and clutching a huge mud-colored fish with both hands, a wild-eyed look on his face. The fish looked as though it was trying to go for his throat.

Ned clicked the mouse and a new image appeared. This one showed only his father's legs and feet, sticking up in the air. The rest of him was over the side of the boat. The fish was leaping to freedom.

I burst out laughing. "Oh, no! He fell overboard?"

"He fell overboard," Ned confirmed. "It took me twenty minutes to fish him out. No pun intended. And that was the end of our great expedition."

"Was he okay?" I asked, taking a sip of my latte.

"He was fine. No injuries. Just wounded pride," Ned said. "Oh, and he had a scare because he had the diamond bracelet he bought my mom for her birthday in his jacket pocket, and he was afraid it might have fallen out. But he got lucky."

"He took a *diamond bracelet* on a fishing trip? In his *pocket*?" I exclaimed.

Ned waved a hand in the air. "You know my dad. He can be kind of nuts sometimes. My mom always goes through all his stuff looking for her present, and he says the only way he can keep it a surprise is just to carry it with him at all times."

"Yeah, but still . . ." I shook my head, appalled. "That's a big risk."

"Tell me about it," Ned agreed. "I think maybe after what happened yesterday he'll be more careful, though. He was really worried there for a minute."

He leaned back in his seat and looked at his watch. "We should get going," he told me. I'd been invited to eat over at the Nickersons' that evening. "Mom's making grilled salmon, I think."

He packed up his laptop and we headed to my car. "After yesterday, will your father ever eat fish again?" I asked with a grin.

"He complained, but Mom told him he has to get back on the fish that threw him," Ned answered. "Anyway, at least it's not catfish."

We stopped off at the market to pick up a nice loaf of bread, and then headed to the Nickersons' house, which was on a pleasant, leafy street in the older section of River Heights. I followed Ned up the walkway and waited while he got out his keys. He slid his key into the keyhole, then frowned.

"That's funny. The door isn't locked," he said as he swung it open. "Mom's usually a fanatic about that." He raised his voice and called, "Mom?"

No one answered. "Mom?" he called again, striding into the kitchen. "You home?"

Still no answer. "Maybe she just ran out for a second," I suggested.

"Could be," Ned said. "I'm going to quickly check upstairs. Maybe she's resting or something."

I followed him up the stairs. Together we peered into the master bedroom. It was quiet and empty, the setting sun turning the white carpet orange.

Ned shrugged. "I guess she must have gone out and forgotten to lock up," he said. "I'm just going to dump my stuff in my room."

He opened the door to his room, which was at the other end of the hallway. Then I heard him gasp. "No!"

My heart thudded. I ran down the hall and peered over his shoulder as he stood frozen in the doorway. My mouth fell open in shock.

There on Ned's bedroom floor lay his mother. Her eyes were closed, her face white. And she wasn't moving.

2

Break-In!

Mom!" Ned exclaimed. He dropped to his knees and grabbed his mother's hand. Her eyelids fluttered and she groaned.

I already had my phone out. I quickly dialed 911. After a moment the dispatcher came on. "What is your emergency?" she asked.

"We need an ambulance right away. A woman is unconscious, maybe with a concussion," I explained. I gave Ned's address, and the dispatcher put me on hold. A moment later she came back on the line.

"The paramedics should be there in four minutes," she told me. "Don't move her until they get there."

"Got it," I said, and hung up.

Edith Nickerson's eyes opened slowly. "Oooh," she said in a faint voice. "What happened?"

"That's what we're wondering," Ned told her, his voice shaky with relief. "Take it easy and just stay put, Mom. The paramedics are on the way. You were unconscious. Did you fall or something?"

A frown pulled Mrs. Nickerson's brows together. "I don't think so. . . ." Then her eyes widened. "No! Ned, there was someone in the house! I heard a noise in your room and I came in to see what it was and—and someone hit me!"

I couldn't stifle my gasp of shock. A burglar? That was seriously creepy.

Ned was already reaching for his phone. He called the police and told them there'd been a break-in. Then he called his father at the office to let him know what had happened.

Mrs. Nickerson squinted at Ned's digital clock. "It was only about fifteen minutes ago," she told me. "I'd just turned on the evening news when I heard the noise." She let out a little gasp. "Nancy, do you think he could still be in the house?"

"No," I said, trying to sound confident. "There was no sign of any disturbance in the rest of the house. Plus the front door was unlocked. I think he got spooked after what he did and just took off."

Ned opened his closet and pulled out his wooden baseball bat "Just in case," he said quietly to me.

"He must have climbed up the elm and come

12

through my window," he went on. "It's been so warm, I've been leaving it open." I glanced across the room and saw that the window was indeed open. A mild autumn breeze stirred the curtains.

Suddenly Mrs. Nickerson gasped again. "My bracelet!" she cried. "My new diamond bracelet! What if he was after that? Ned, go check in my bedside table. Please tell me it's still there!"

Ned ran down the hall to his parents' room. A moment later he returned, holding a black velvet jewelry case. "It's still here," he said.

"Oh, thank goodness," Mrs. Nickerson breathed.

The doorbell pealed, announcing the arrival of the paramedics. "I'll get it," I said, and hurried downstairs to let them in.

The police pulled up just as I opened the door, and two uniformed officers immediately started checking the house. One of them was my friend, Ellen Johansen. I was glad to see her.

"No one here," she reported as she came into Ned's room a few moments later. "Ma'am, can you describe what happened?"

By now the paramedics had helped Mrs. Nickerson to Ned's desk chair, where she was sitting and arguing with them about whether or not she should go to the hospital for overnight observation. "Don't be ridiculous. I'm perfectly fine," she said briskly.

"But, ma'am, any head trauma is potentially very serious," one of the paramedics said. "It's our responsibility to get you checked out."

"I'm telling you, I'm all right. My vision isn't blurred, I can remember everything perfectly, and I'm not in the least nauseated. If it makes you feel any better, I promise to go to my doctor in the morning. But the last thing I want to do right now is spend the night in a hospital bed," Mrs. Nickerson said. "You might as well stop trying, because I'm not going to change my mind."

The paramedics looked unhappy. I grinned at Ned. Mrs. Nickerson was sounding a lot more like herself.

"Ma'am?" Officer Johansen, who had been waiting patiently, repeated. "Can you describe what happened?"

I listened as Mrs. Nickerson went through her story. "It was just six o'clock," she said. "I'd come upstairs to get something and I heard a noise in Ned's room. I went in to see what it was, and someone hit me on the back of the head."

"Did you get a look at this person?" Officer Johansen asked, writing in her notebook.

"No, I'm afraid I didn't see him at all. When I came in, the room looked empty. He must have been behind the door," Mrs. Nickerson told her.

"Mmm. Anything missing?" Officer Johansen asked.

"I don't think so," Mrs. Nickerson began. But then

Ned, who'd been opening and closing his desk drawers with a troubled expression, interrupted.

"Yes, there is. My digital camera," he said. "I left it sitting on my desk this morning. It's gone."

"Oh, no!" I said. That camera was Ned's baby. It was brand new and super deluxe. It practically took pictures by itself. He'd spent weeks researching exactly what he wanted and months working extra hours at his campus job to save the money for it.

"Oh, honey, I'm sorry," Ned's mom said. "Fortunately, our insurance will pay for the replacement." She turned back to Officer Johansen, who'd been joined by her partner, a short man with a crew cut whose name tag said HINKLEY. "I think I know what the thief was after," she said, and held up the velvet jewelry box with the bracelet in it. "My husband gave me this yesterday for my birthday. I wore it out to dinner last night and I'm afraid I showed it off quite a bit. My guess is that someone in the restaurant saw me flashing it and followed us home."

"Could be," Officer Hinkley said in a noncommittal tone. He examined the open window. "This how he got in?"

"I guess so," Mrs. Nickerson said.

"You leave your windows open as a habit?" he asked, making it sound as though getting some fresh air was just short of a crime.

"It's never been a problem before," Ned said, bristling.

"We think the burglar left by the front door, though," I put in. "It was unlocked when Ned and I got here. It might be worth knocking on a few doors. It's a long shot, but maybe one of the neighbors saw him leaving."

I was trying to be polite and not act like I was telling the police how to do their job. I've had a few run-ins with Pete McGinnis, the chief of police. He's basically a good guy, and he runs a great police department, but he tends to get testy when I solve mysteries his people can't.

Now Officer Hinkley looked me up and down. "I've seen you at headquarters. You're Nancy Drew, aren't you?" he asked. "The teenage detective?"

The way he said it, I could practically see the air quotes around the word *detective*. But I just smiled politely. "Yes, that's me."

"Hmm. Maybe you should leave police work to the police," he said.

My smile froze, but Officer Johansen cut in before I could say anything.

"Thanks for the tip," she said. "We'll talk to the neighbors, but it's true, it is a long shot. We'll let you know if we find out anything useful." She glanced at her partner with a slight frown. "Come on, Carl."

After they and the paramedics left, Ned and I helped his mother down the stairs. In the living room she put her feet up on the couch. I propped pillows behind her while Ned brought her an ice pack and some aspirin.

"Thanks, Ned. I didn't want to tell those paramedics, or they'd probably have rushed me off to surgery, but my head really does hurt," Mrs. Nickerson admitted. "I don't know that I'm up to cooking dinner tonight. I'm sorry."

"Oh, please! As if anyone would expect you to, after what happened to you!" I exclaimed.

"Nancy and I can cook," Ned volunteered.

I caught Mrs. Nickerson's horrified look and burst out laughing. "I don't think that's a good idea," I told Ned. "Remember when we cooked for your parents on their anniversary? We're just lucky no one ended up in the hospital after that meal! You can barely boil water, and I'm worse. How about we just order a couple of pizzas?"

"That sounds perfect, Nancy," Mrs. Nickerson said gratefully. She sighed. "You know, I didn't get the impression that Officer Hinkley is all that eager to track down this burglar."

"Neither did I," Ned agreed, scowling.

"Well," I pointed out, "to be fair, I don't know how much the police can do beyond talking to your neighbors. If no one saw anything—and I doubt anybody did, especially since it was the time of day when most people are in the kitchen getting dinner ready—that's pretty much the end of it, as far as the police are concerned."

"But what about all those people at the restaurant?" Mrs. Nickerson protested. "I'm sure I'm right about someone being after my bracelet. Can't they get a list of the people who were there last night and investigate them?"

"Not really," I said. "I mean, they could interview them, but without some kind of evidence that links someone to this house, they can't really go beyond questions, and I don't think that would accomplish much. What restaurant was it, by the way?"

"Al di La," Mrs. Nickerson told me. "That Officer Hinkley didn't even ask me that!"

At that point James Nickerson barreled through the door, demanding to know what had happened. While Mrs. Nickerson was giving the details, Ned and I went into the kitchen to order pizzas.

"You know," Ned said thoughtfully as he hung up the phone, "there's someone else who saw Mom's bracelet. The guy at the marina where Dad and I rented the boat yesterday—I think his name is Lonny. Big guy, with long hair. When we got back to shore and Dad was dripping wet, of course he wanted to know what had happened. Dad gave him the blow-by-blow and even showed him the bracelet. Lonny was pretty impressed with it. He kept asking if the diamonds were real."

"Huh," I said. "And he wouldn't need to follow you home to find out where you live. He'd have all that info from the paperwork you had to fill out to rent the boat."

"Exactly," Ned agreed.

"You didn't mention that to the police," I pointed out.

Ned shrugged. "Like you said, there's not much they can do without evidence. And I figured, since that's true, maybe it's not a good idea for them to go asking questions and letting Lonny know that he's a suspect."

"Aha," I said, my eyebrows rising as I realized where he was going. "But if, say, a girl was to stop by the marina tomorrow and ask this Lonny a few questions about her boyfriend's crazy boating adventure last Sunday, it probably wouldn't occur to him that she might be fishing for other information. Right?"

"That's what I like about you," Ned said, kissing the tip of my nose. "You're a girl who knows how to pick up a hint."

I felt a little glow, and it wasn't just from Ned's kiss. My detective sense was tingling. I had the feeling I was about to start my next case!

3

Trolling for a Thief

When the pizza arrived we all ate it sitting around the coffee table in the living room. "Ahh, I feel much better now," Mrs. Nickerson said as she finished a slice with pepperoni and mushrooms. "Thanks, Ned and Nancy, for taking such good care of me. I'm sorry I wasn't able to cook—I had such a nice salmon dinner planned."

"Actually," Ned said, helping himself to a third slice, "I have a theory."

"Oh?" I said. "What's that?"

He grinned. "I think the entire break-in was part of a plot by Dad to prevent Mom from cooking fish and thus reminding him of his moment of shame on the river yesterday."

"I object to that remark!" Ned's father protested.

"Falling into the water is a time-honored part of fishing. Anyway, if I'd planned the break-in I would have stolen the salmon itself."

We all laughed at that. Then, sobering, Mr. Nickerson went on, "Seriously, though, I'm just glad you got off with only a bump on the head, dear." He took Mrs. Nickerson's hand in his. "It could have been much worse. I guess we always think these kinds of thing happen to other people—until they happen to us, that is."

Mrs. Nickerson nodded emphatically. "That's so true. You know, I always imagined thieves struck in the dead of night. But this one just came in, in broad daylight, as bold as brass. And walked out the front door as if he had nothing to hide. It's frightening!"

"It is kind of strange," I agreed, frowning. "The fact is, many burglars try to hit a place during the day, while people are likely to be at work. But I've never heard of anyone trying to break in right around dinnertime."

"It doesn't make a lot of sense, does it?" Mr. Nickerson said. "But I guess if burglars had more sense, they wouldn't be burglars."

"I asked Nancy to do some investigating," Ned told his parents. "And not just because I'm bummed out about my brand-new camera either. Maybe if we figure out who broke in, we'll be able to make sure it doesn't happen again."

"Well, Nancy, I've seen you in action and so I know I don't need to tell you to be careful," Mrs. Nickerson said. Her brow creased. "But all the same: Please be careful, dear."

"I will be," I assured her, feeling a rush of warmth. Ned and I have been together for such a long time that his mom is a little like a mother to me, too, especially since I lost my own mother when I was only three years old.

After we finished eating, Ned and I went upstairs and I used his computer to put together a list of all the pawnshops in River Heights and the suburbs. "I figure the thief will want to pawn your camera," I explained to him. "He could probably get a couple of hundred dollars for it. If I can find it in one of the pawnshops, then maybe I'll be able discover who took it there."

"You're cute when you talk shop," Ned said, tucking a wisp of my strawberry blond hair behind my ear.

"You know, there are a surprising number of pawnbrokers in River Heights," I commented as I scanned the screen. "I mean, it's not a big city."

"Yeah, but it's colorful," Ned pointed out. "It's a town that started with a heist, remember? The Rackham Gang, back in the eighteen hundreds? And there are certainly plenty of crooks nowadays, too."

"Yeah, good point," I said, laughing. "Anyway, I

guess I've got my work cut out for me tomorrow."

When we went back down, Ned's parents were watching the news. The anchorwoman was reporting on the upcoming election for governor. "The Baxter campaign today called again for an investigation of Solomon Paper's role in the high levels of chlorine compounds that have recently been detected in several species of river fish. Richard Solomon vigorously defended his company's environmental record."

The screen changed to show a shot of Richard Solomon standing in front of the Solomon Paper plant, which was located a few miles outside of River Heights. Solomon was tall, with graying dark hair swept back from a broad forehead.

"The claim that Solomon Paper has anything to do with these pollutants that have been found is ridiculous," he was saying. "First of all, we phased out all use of chlorine bleach more than ten years ago. Seventy percent of our paper is made from recycled pulp, and the rest is made using chlorine-free bleaches. Second, we are a zero-discharge mill, meaning that we do not dump anything at all into this river or any other water system. Solomon Paper is the most environmentally friendly paper company you will ever find. Frankly, this is nothing but a witch hunt by the Baxter campaign because we're ahead in the polls. Shame on them for using such tactics."

"All right!" Ned cheered. "That's telling them!"

"What does the *Bugle* say?" I asked Ned's dad. "Is it going to back Richard Solomon for governor?" As James Nickerson was the publisher of the *River Heights Bugle*, I knew he'd be writing an editorial endorsing one of the candidates. But even though Ned was volunteering on Solomon's campaign, Mr. Nickerson still hadn't made up his mind whom to back. Ned had been working hard to convince his dad that Solomon was the right choice.

"Well, Raelene Baxter has more experience in state government, obviously, since she's been lieutenant governor for the last eight years," Mr. Nickerson said. He shook his head. "But Richard Solomon has some very interesting ideas. And he's right about the Baxter campaign and this pollution issue. The *Bugle* has been looking into Solomon Paper's environmental record, and as far as I can see, they're squeaky clean—at least since Richard Solomon took over from his father."

"What about before?" I asked.

He shrugged. "That was the bad old days, before the government cracked down on companies that polluted the environment. But old Mr. Solomon didn't have the greatest reputation, I'll say that. Apparently his motto was 'profit, profit, profit,' and he didn't much care how he got it."

"Sounds like a wonderful human being," Mrs. Nickerson said with a wry smile.

I checked my watch. It was already past nine. "I'd better head home," I said. "If I'm going to go running at six in the morning, I need my beauty sleep!"

"Thanks again, Nancy dear, for being here and taking such wonderful care of me," Ned's mother said.

"You're welcome," I replied, bending down to give her a hug.

As I drove home I started making a list in my head of the first steps I needed to take in my new case. First of all I wanted to talk to anyone Ned or his parents thought might be a suspect. That list so far included only Lonny, the boat boy. Second, I would visit the local pawnshops and see if Ned's camera had turned up anywhere.

Of course, I thought, we could be wrong about the burglar's motive. Maybe whoever it was had just picked the Nickersons' house at random, not even knowing about Mrs. Nickerson's diamond bracelet. Still, the idea that someone was after the bracelet seemed like a good place to start.

I pulled into the driveway and let myself into my house, which was quiet and dark. My dad, who's a criminal defense lawyer, was away at a conference in San Francisco. And Hannah Gruen, our live-in housekeeper, had already gone to bed.

I'd better do the same, I thought. Tomorrow is going to be a long day!

"I'm going to die," Bess moaned. "Can we please . . . take a water break?"

"We've only jogged for three minutes so far," I pointed out.

"That can't . . . be right," Bess panted. "It feels . . . like an . . . hour!"

True to her word, George had knocked on my kitchen door at five minutes before six that morning, Bess in tow. Bess was decked out in distressed jersey shorts with a designer logo across the rear, a matching hoodie, and pink-and-silver running shoes. George proudly showed off the heart-rate monitor strapped around her torso, as well as the odometer she wore clipped to her waistband to measure her distance and pace. "Let's go!" she said. She clapped her hands together. "This is going to be great!"

"Yeah, right. Hey, Nancy," Bess said as I hurried out the door, twisting my strawberry blond hair into a scrunchie with one hand while cramming the last of a piece of toast into my mouth with the other. "You know, your sweatpants are on inside out."

I glanced down. Whoops! Bess was right—the fuzzy part was on the outside of my navy sweats.

"I'm starting a new style," I said with a shrug.

"It's called 'throw your clothes on in thirty seconds in the dark.'"

"I'm scared," Bess whispered as George bounded off down the street. "No one should have so much energy at this time of the day. I swear there's something wrong with her!"

I grinned. "Let's just make sure we stick together, okay?"

It was a humid, gray morning, with shreds of fog just starting to break up in the daylight. George, who was already about twenty yards in front of us, circled back and fell into step beside me. "Let's pick up the pace, guys!" She turned so that she was jogging backward. "We'll take a water break at the end of the second mile, and do some crunches and push-ups while we're getting our heart rates down."

"The *second* mile?" I said. "Uh, George, how many miles are you planning for us to run?"

"Don't worry, I'm starting us off slowly. Only three miles today," George said. "I figure we'll work our way up to four by the weekend, and then next week, we'll get up to five, then six the following week. Plus we'll do some intervals and hill-sprints for speed, and of course calisthenics for overall muscle tone. And I've got this high-protein diet we can follow—"

"Diet? Calesthenics? Hill-sprints?" I glared at her. What made everything so much worse was that she

27

wasn't even slightly out of breath. "George, this isn't the Olympics!"

"No, but we can pretend it is," George said happily.

"But Bess has never run before! And I haven't run in a long time! We need to ease into it more gradually. Bess, help me out here!" I said, turning to her. "Why aren't you arguing?"

Bess's face was practically the same shade of magenta as her hoodie. "No . . . breath," she gasped. "Sorry."

"Suck it up!" George called. "Run through the pain!" She lengthened her stride and pulled ahead of us.

"I'm going to kill her," I grumbled. "Is that okay with you, Bess?"

I glanced at Bess. She couldn't spare the breath to answer, but she gave me a thumbs-up.

Soon I was feeling pretty breathless myself. Plus I had a mild cramp in my calf. But then I noticed that the route George had chosen was leading down to the river's edge. Not only was it beautiful—a gravel trail wound along the riverbank, and the morning air was cool and soft—but it also led directly to the River Heights Country Club golf course. Which happened to be right next to the marina where my chief—well, to be honest, my *only*—suspect works! Score!

With an effort, I lengthened my stride to catch up with George. "We need . . . to take a break," I puffed. "Turn left . . . at the marina . . . entrance."

George consulted her odometer. "But that's only a mile," she said.

I gave her a look. "George. We're dying. You keep going . . . if you want."

George made a face. "Okay, okay. But I know you're only doing this because you want to talk to the marina guy. You aren't fooling me." I'd brought my friends up to speed on my new case in an e-mail last night.

I grinned. "You know me too well," I said.

She turned left down the marina driveway. Bess and I followed. The driveway was unpaved and covered with deep ruts, which were full of water from last night's rain. I heard Bess squawk as she splashed through one by accident. "My shoe!"

I turned to glance over my shoulder at her. The next thing I knew, my sneaker was slipping out from under me on a muddy patch. Oh no! I was going down!

4

All Wet

SPLASH! I landed on my rear end in a puddle. Brown goo fountained up around me.

"Oh, ugghhh!" I gasped. I scrambled to my feet as quickly as I could, but the damage was done. My sweats were soaked through, and I was spattered with mud from head to toe.

"Nan, are you okay?" Bess cried. Pulling off her sweatshirt, she dabbed at me with it.

"Wow, that was a spectacular fall!" George added. I could tell that she was trying hard not to smile. I glared at her for a second, but I couldn't keep it up. I burst out laughing. In a moment, all three of us were giggling like crazy people.

"Well, I don't know how this is going to affect my

investigation," I said. "What do you think—do I look like a damsel in distress?"

"You look more like a damsel in dah mud," Bess said, and started cracking up again.

As the three of us walked toward the marina, George sniffed the air and wrinkled her nose. "Ugh. What is that awful smell?"

"George!" Bess scolded. "It's not Nancy's fault! It's the mud."

But by then I'd caught a whiff of the odor too. It was faint but horrible—like a combination of stinky gym socks and rotten food. "Thanks for defending me, but I don't think it's the mud," I said. "I've smelled that smell once before, when we went on that volunteer trip to that swamp, remember, where there was a toxic waste dump and we had to rescue the ducks?"

"You mean that smell is toxic waste?" Bess cried. "That's terrible!"

"I don't know if it's toxic waste or if it's something else, like swamp gas," I said. "But, you know, there have been a lot of stories in the news recently about high levels of pollution in the river."

"It's a crime," George said flatly. "If some company is dumping their toxic waste in the river, they should all go to jail."

We were all silent for a moment. I agreed with George. I hated the thought of someone carelessly poisoning our gorgeous river.

The marina was a shabby little place, with five rickety wooden docks reaching out into the river. Eight or nine boats were tied up in slips, but most of the slips were empty. The office was a single-story cinder-block building set on the most distant dock. Tied alongside it was an ancient, rusty fishing trawler piled high with cement mooring blocks.

As we approached the office, the door opened and a tall, thin man in blue work overalls stepped out, carrying a toolbox. He squinted at us. "Can I help you girls?" he asked in a gravelly voice.

"We were wondering if we could use your rest-room. I had a little accident in the mud," I said, indicating my filthy outfit with a wave of my hand.

"It's around the other side. I'll have to unlock it for you. This way," he said over his shoulder as he started off around the corner of the building.

"We'll wait here," George called after me as I followed.

"Thanks, I really appreciate it, Mr., uh . . . ," I said, hurrying to keep up with the man's long stride.

"Snead. Bill Snead. I run the marina," he told me.

"Nice to meet you, Mr. Snead. I'm Nancy Drew. I

was also looking for Lonny," I added. "Is he working today?"

"He'll be in at seven," Mr. Snead said. "Something I can help you with?"

"I don't think so," I said. "See, Lonny rented a boat to my boyfriend and his dad on Sunday morning and I wanted to talk to him about that."

"Sunday morning?" Mr. Snead said, halting to look at me. "What time?"

"Oh, really early," I said, a little surprised. "Like five a.m."

He frowned. "I was here Sunday morning. What do you want to know?"

"Um, well—" My mind raced as I tried to come up with an innocent-sounding question that only Lonny could answer. "Well, last night Ned showed me a bunch of pictures from the fishing trip and in one of them it looked like Lonny had a cool belt-clip case for his cell phone, and I wanted to ask where he got it so I could get one for Ned. Our anniversary is coming up."

After a moment he shrugged, fished out his key ring, and unlocked the restroom door. "Guess you're right, I can't help you with that. Like I said, Lonny'll be in at seven. You can wait for him if you want."

"Thanks again," I said, and stepped inside to wash up.

I peered at myself in the streaked mirror over the sink. My eyes looked bluer than usual against the big smear of mud on my cheek. Luckily my hair had miraculously stayed unsplashed. I washed my face and hands and took the scrunchie out of my hair, shaking it so that it fell around my face. There. With my cheeks still pink from the run, I looked halfway decent. That is, if you could ignore my muddy clothes, which nothing short of the "heavy soil" cycle on the washing machine could fix.

When I went back around to the front of the building, George and Bess were already in conversation with a guy who looked like he was around our age. He was beefy, with longish brown hair, and he wore jeans and a white muscle shirt. Lonny, I guessed from the description Ned had given me the night before. Luckily for me, he'd arrived early. As is usually the case with guys, Lonny obviously couldn't keep his eyes off Bess.

"You look much better," Bess greeted me. "Nancy, this is Lonny. Lonny was just telling us about his band."

"Nice to meet you," I said. "Actually, I was hoping I could find you. My boyfriend, Ned Nickerson, was here with his dad on Sunday. Maybe you remember them. Ned's dad fell in the river?"

Lonny let out a guffaw. "Oh, yeah, that guy. He

was carrying a diamond bracelet in his pocket too. What a dimwit."

"Right," I said, keeping the smile on my face, though his comment annoyed me. "Well, anyway, I wanted to ask you . . ."

Mr. Snead, who was sorting coils of rope on the dock nearby, glanced up. I hadn't been planning to use that lame story about the cell phone case, but I didn't want to change it if he was listening. So I went through it again.

"Cell phone case?" Lonny shook his head. "I don't use a case. Carry my phone in my pocket." He fished it out to show me.

"Huh, that's weird," I said, trying to sound innocent and puzzled. "Well, I guess it must have been a funny shadow on the photo or something."

"You got the picture on you?" Lonny asked. "Maybe I could figure out what it was you saw."

"No, sorry," I told him. "I don't have a hard copy— I saw it on Ned's laptop." I paused, wondering how on earth I was going to change the subject to what he'd been doing the night before. Then I had an idea. "So what's your band called?" I asked.

His eyes lit up. "Bucket of Blood," he said proudly. "We rock! I play lead guitar."

"Bucket of Blood?" Bess made a face.

"Oh, I think I've heard of you guys!" I said, giving

him a big smile. "Didn't you play a show at the university last night? I thought I saw a poster for you on a bulletin board there."

"No, it wasn't us," Lonny said, and his face fell. "We're, uh, still shopping our demo disc around. You know, looking for exactly the right gigs."

Mr. Snead snorted. Picking up his coils of rope, he climbed aboard the old fishing trawler.

"Translation: They can't get booked anywhere," George whispered behind me. I kicked her discreetly. I didn't want to upset Lonny.

Then Lonny added, "But if you want to hear us, you can come check us out anytime. We practice in my cousin's garage every Monday and Thursday at six. It's over on Elm Grove Road. Four fourteen Elm Grove."

"Monday and Thursday at six?" I repeated. "Did you practice last night?"

"Oh, yeah. We never miss a jam," Lonny assured me.

Hmm. That meant he couldn't have been breaking into the Nickersons' house yesterday at six, unless he was lying. "Isn't six kind of early to play rock?"

"It's the only time we have," Lonny explained. "My cousin doesn't get home from work till five thirty, and my aunt won't let us play after eight. She says it annoys the neighbors. I say, if they aren't rocking with us, who cares if they're annoyed?" He sighed. "But my aunt is pretty hard to argue with."

"Huh," I said absently. I would drive over to Elm Grove Road and double-check what he had told me, of course, but I had a feeling he was telling the truth. That meant he couldn't be the mystery burglar. "Well, thanks, anyway."

"For what?" Lonny asked, looking puzzled.

"Uh . . . for . . . for telling us about your band," I improvised. "We'll keep an eye out for you."

"Oh, definitely," Bess chimed in. "Bucket of Blood."

"Not a name you can forget," George added.

Lonny beamed. "It's good, isn't it? Why don't you girls give me your e-mail addresses and I'll put you on our mailing list. We got a website and everything."

A look of panic crossed Bess's face. "Uh, that sounds great," I said quickly. "But we, um, don't have any paper on us." I gestured at our running outfits with an apologetic smile. "Why don't you just tell me the name of your website and I'll e-mail you with all our info when I get home. Which I have got to do before all this mud dries on me."

"Oh, okay." Lonny looked disappointed. "It's BucketofBlood.com."

"Of course," George murmured.

"Thanks again. Let's go, guys," I said, turning to Bess and George.

"Bye," Bess said as we headed back up the driveway.

"Later," Lonny called.

"So, he's not your burglar, huh?" George asked as soon as we were out of sight of the marina.

I shook my head. "Doesn't look like he could have done it. Oh, well, it's always good to cross a suspect off the list. I just wish my list was a little longer."

"Ow," Bess grumbled. "My leg hurts. I think I pulled a ligament or strained a tendon or something."

"I think it's called *muscle use*," George teased. "Look, you guys, I'm letting you off easy because it's our first day."

"We know," Bess said.

"We're sorry," I added.

"All I'm saying is, you'd better get psyched, because we're going to do the whole distance tomorrow." With that, George picked up her pace to a fast, effortless jog. "See you later!" she called over her shoulder. "Don't forget to stretch!"

"She's a slave driver," I muttered as we watched her go.

"But we love her, anyway," Bess said with a grin.

As we headed off toward my house, it began to drizzle.

"Oh, perfect. I'm going back to bed," Bess announced.

For a second I felt like doing exactly the same thing, but I couldn't. I had to get going on my day. Even though my only firm suspect didn't seem to be panning out, there was still a lot of legwork I could do to move this case along. There were pawnshops to visit, restaurant workers to interview . . .

As I started planning, I felt a familiar excitement bubble up inside me. It's the feeling I get whenever I've got a good mystery on my hands. I was ready to get to work!

Snagged

I felt much better after I stretched, took a shower, and put on clean clothes. When I went down to the kitchen, Hannah was setting two places at the breakfast table. The smells of bacon and fresh-squeezed orange juice swirled through the air, and my stomach instantly started to grumble.

"Yum, that smells so good!" I exclaimed. "What can I do to help?"

"You can sit yourself down and eat," Hannah told me. "What with your father being away at that conference and you having your busy life, I feel as if I've been living in a ghost house! I need to feed you just to make sure you're real." Smiling to take the sting out of her words, she bustled over and set a heaping plate of bacon, eggs, and fresh-baked blueberry muffins in front of me.

"Sorry you've been abandoned," I said, reaching up to give her a one-armed hug. "But I haven't been having pure fun, believe me. I've got a new mystery to solve." I told her about the burglary at the Nickersons'.

Hannah listened, shaking her head in sympathy. "Poor Mrs. Nickerson," she said. "I'm going to take her a basket of muffins. And I think I'll just whip up a pot of chicken soup in case she's feeling bad again today."

I smiled. Hannah's remedy for whatever ails you is always food. She's the best cook I know, though, so her method works more often than you might think.

I finished my breakfast, cleared my dishes, and then headed out to my car. By now it was about ten o'clock in the morning—too early for the restaurant where the Nickersons had eaten to be open, but not too early, I hoped, for some useful gossip. For that I had a great source: Harold Safer.

Harold owns Safer's Cheese shop, the best place for cheese in River Heights (or, as Harold insists, the best place for cheese in the entire Midwest). He knows everything about food—and everything about all the restaurants and food people in the town.

The electronic bell on the door played the first few notes of "The Sound of Music" as I walked into his shop. Harold glanced up from the counter, where he was serving a woman, and gave me a wave, his round face breaking into a smile. "Nancy! Give me a minute, doll face. You have to hear my new recording of *The Phantom of the Opera*. It will give you chills, I promise!"

The other thing Harold knows everything—and I do mean *everything*—about is musical theater. He can sing you any song from any Broadway show, even the ones that no one else has ever heard of. He travels to New York at least twice a year just to see the new productions.

He finished ringing up his customer's purchases and she left. "How's business?" I asked.

He made a face. "Slow, slow, slow. Yesterday I only had six customers all day. If it wasn't for my restaurant supply sideline, I'd be worried."

"Oh, don't worry. Business will pick up in a few days," I assured him. "You know it always does. Anyway, I'm glad you're not so busy right now. I was hoping you'd have a little time for gossip."

Harold's eyes lit up behind his glasses. He perched on his stool and put his elbows on the counter, resting his chin in his cupped hands. "I always have time for gossip. Who are we talking about?"

"Well, you supply cheese to Al di La, don't you?" I asked. Al di La was the restaurant where the Nickersons had eaten on Sunday night.

"That's right," Harold confirmed. "Fabulous food, but oh, sister, look out for Rocco Vitale. You know, the chef-owner of the place. He's a madman! My friend Lorna landed a job as a waitress there a few months ago. She was surprised the job was so easy to get, since the place is so popular. Well, she found out why." He paused dramatically.

I leaned forward. "Why?" I asked.

Harold pursed his lips. "Lorna lasted all of three nights. The first two nights Rocco yelled at her so much, she cried herself to sleep. The third night he actually waved a cleaver at her. That's when she quit. Now she's working at Gelly's Steakhouse. The tips aren't as good, but at least she isn't being threatened with sharp objects."

Hmm. As interesting as this was, it didn't sound like it was going to help me solve my mystery. "I don't suppose this Rocco Vitale has a record for burglary, does he?" I asked halfheartedly.

"I doubt it," Harold said. "He's more of a crime-of-passion type of person."

"I see. And do you know any of the people who work in the restaurant?"

Harold shook his head. "Just Lorna, but she's not

there anymore. I think it's mostly students from the university who are trying to make some extra cash."

I sighed. "Well, I have to say, this case isn't exactly off to a running start. I guess I'd better start making the rounds of the pawnshops."

"Pawnshops!" Harold cried. "Ooh, ooh, Nancy, can I please go with you? I promise I'll be good and not get in your way. I just love the idea of going to a pawnshop. It's so retro!" He hurried into the back and returned a moment later carrying a khaki trench coat. "I've even got the perfect outfit for it!"

I hid a smile. "Harold, you know you missed your calling. You should have been an actor."

"Don't think I haven't thought about it," Harold told me. "I could see myself on Broadway, couldn't you?" He pulled on his trench coat, belted it around his waist, checked his reflection in the long mirror behind the counter, then came around to join me. "But if you want to know the truth, I'm too chicken to try out. I went to an audition last year in New York and when the time came for me to get up there and sing, I just couldn't do it." He flipped the sign on the door to read CLOSED, then held the door open and ushered me out. "Anyway, I love cheese almost as much as I love a good Broadway tune, so I'm doing all right here in River Heights."

The first pawnshop we went to was on the far end

of State Street, near Jeffries Autorama. Harold had popped his *Phantom of the Opera* CD into my car stereo, and as I turned off the ignition, the throbbing strains of Raoul and Christine singing "Think of Me" died away, to my secret relief. I prefer something with more of a beat.

I pushed open the pawnshop door and glanced around. It was a small room, with a row of TVs and stereos on a shelf behind the counter. Bracelets, rings, necklaces, and cuff links sparkled in a satin-lined glass display case. There were a few digital cameras and other small electronic items in another glass case to the right of the door. None of them looked like Ned's, but I knew that pawnshops often kept more items in the back, only displaying the ones that were up for resale.

"Can I help you?" asked the heavyset man behind the counter.

I held out the notes Ned had written down for me about the camera's make and model. "I'm looking for one of these," I told him. "Do you have any?"

The man glanced at the paper, then shook his head and handed it back. "Nope. All I got in digital cameras is what you see here."

Harold stepped up to the counter and leaned over it. "Listen, pal," he growled. "Do yourself a favor and don't lie to the lady, if you know what's good for you, see?"

"Excuse me?" the man said, looking startled.

"I just—," I began, but Harold cut me off.

"Let me handle this," he said to me, and my jaw dropped as I realized that he was putting on a voice like someone from one of those old black-and-white gangster movies. He leaned farther over the counter and grabbed the pawnshop owner by his collar. "I think you understand me," he snarled. "Now go in the back and get the goods for the lady, or else."

"'Or else'?" repeated the pawnshop owner. "Or else what? Listen, buddy, I don't know who you think you are, but you're wrinkling my shirt. Are you going to let go, or should I call the cops?"

"Harold!" I finally managed. I grabbed his arm and pulled him away from the counter. "Sorry," I said to the pawnshop owner. "He's just joking. Aren't you, Harold?" Gripping his arm firmly, I steered him out of the pawnshop as quickly as I could.

"What on earth were you doing in there?" I demanded when we were out on the sidewalk.

"Not what, who," Harold corrected me. "That was my Edward G. Robinson impression. Not bad, eh?"

"I don't know about that," I said. "What I do know is that you can't go around grabbing people by their collars and threatening them, Harold! Honestly!"

"But it was a pawnshop!" he protested. "A seedy place full of shady characters and stolen goods!"

"Maybe in the old movies you watch," I told him. "But things have changed, Harold. Pawnshops are very strictly regulated now. The owners have to supply lists of their inventory, complete with make, model, and serial number, to the police every day. If they suspect something is stolen property, they report it. They're businesspeople, not criminals. Okay, maybe some of them aren't as careful as they should be about who they buy things from, but mostly they can't afford to break the law."

"Oh," Harold said. He thought about it for a moment. "That's not nearly as interesting as my version. Life in black and white was just so much more colorful."

I laughed. "Sorry to disappoint you," I said. "Now, how about in the next shop you leave the talking to me?"

Harold gave me a mock salute. "You're the boss, boss."

We went to four more pawnshops, and Harold managed to behave himself in all of them, but none of them had a camera like Ned's. By that time, it was after one p.m., so Harold and I went back to his shop, where he made us a delicious lunch of bread and cheese with sliced apples and pears.

After that, I had to head over to the River Heights Animal Shelter—I volunteer there once a month.

The vet was there, vaccinating the new puppies, so I held the little yappers while she stuck needles in them. It wasn't pretty, but afterward I got to play with the puppies for a while.

At about six o'clock, I checked my cell phone, which I'd left in my car by accident, and saw that Ned had called twice. There was no message, so I called him back immediately. "Is everything okay? How's your mom doing?" I asked when he answered his phone.

"Better than I am," Ned replied. He sounded frustrated.

"Why? What's up?" I asked.

"I can't believe this week!" Ned groused. "It's only Tuesday, right? That means there's three more days for something to go wrong!"

"Ned," I said, "just tell me what happened."

"Another theft," Ned said. "My laptop was stolen right out from under my nose!"

6

Suspicious Snapshot

Oh no!" I exclaimed. "Your laptop was stolen? Ned, I'm so sorry! You *are* having a terrible week!"

"Tell me about it," Ned said with a sigh. "What's worse, my Victorian poetry paper was on that computer. It's due Friday. Now I'll have to rewrite the whole thing in three days."

"Where are you?" I asked.

"I'm at the Solomon campaign headquarters," Ned answered. "I came here to print out some flyers for the rally on Friday. I'd just set up my computer when all the power in the building went off. Of course there was a ton of confusion and we were all running around trying to figure out what had happened, and when the lights came back on, my computer was gone."

"Did anyone call the police?"

"Yes, they've already come and gone. But what can they do? Once again, no one saw anything."

"I'm on my way," I promised, and hopped into my car. "Maybe there's something I can do to help."

The campaign headquarters were on River Street, on the ground floor of a small brick building that housed an accountant's office. A banner over the plate-glass window in the front read RICHARD SOLOMON FOR GOVERNOR.

I hurried inside and found Ned standing near the door, talking to Richard Solomon and a girl I recognized as Gretchen Hochman, one of Solomon's campaign staffers.

"I'm telling you, it has to be them," she was arguing. "I worked with their campaign manager two years ago, and I know there's no dirty trick he wouldn't pull. The Baxter campaign did this. Count on it!"

"I don't know, Gretchen," Solomon said, shaking his head. "It seems kind of, well, kooky. I mean, a smear campaign is one thing, but vandalism and theft? I just don't see it. No, I think this was the work of some random criminal, nothing more."

I slipped my hand into Ned's and gave it a gentle squeeze. "Hey, Nan," he said with a strained smile. He quickly introduced me to Richard Solomon and Gretchen.

"Nancy Drew." Richard Solomon shook my hand with a warm smile. In person he was younger looking than on TV. And his eyes were a surprising shade of green. "Surely I've heard of you. Aren't you a detective?"

"That's me," I said.

"Nancy has a better track record of solving mysteries than the River Heights Police Department," Ned boasted. "She'll crack the case every time."

"So I've gathered. Chief McGinnis and I play poker together every now and then," Solomon told me. "I've heard him grousing more than once about how you made him look bad." He chuckled. "I think you're good for him."

My cheeks turned pink. Something about the way he looked at me made me feel as if he was really paying full attention. I guess that's called charisma, I thought.

"If you're a detective, maybe you can look into what happened here," Gretchen said. "I know it was the Baxter campaign. I just know it! They're running scared, and they're desperate."

"Gretchen, come on," Solomon protested. "I appreciate your loyalty, but you've got to let this idea go."

"I'd be happy to take a look around," I said, "though I have to say, I agree with Mr. Solomon. It seems unlikely the Baxter campaign would actually resort to crime, no matter how much they're trailing in the polls."

"Come on," Ned said. "I'll walk you through it."

He led me over to a workstation close to the window. "This is where I was working," he explained. "I'd just started printing when the lights went out."

"About what time was this?" I asked.

He shrugged. "Maybe five o'clock."

I frowned as I thought about this. "But it's not fully dark at five at this time of year. What's the point of putting out the lights? I mean, from a burglar's point of view?"

"We had all the blinds closed because the sunset was creating glare on the computers," Ned said. "So actually it went pitch-dark in here."

I nodded. "Okay. So then what?"

"Then we all jumped up and started yelling and running around like idiots, bumping into one another and the furniture," Ned confessed. "Finally Richard found his way to the door, went down to the basement, and flipped the breakers back on. The whole thing probably took about ten minutes."

"Was anything taken besides your computer?" I asked.

"Not as far as I know," Ned answered. "It was the only laptop in here—all the other computers are desktops. But nobody's purse or wallet got taken or anything like that."

"I see," I said. I gazed around the room, my eyes narrowing as I thought. "You know, now that I look at the setup, I can't help wondering if Gretchen might be onto something."

"What, you mean you think the Baxter campaign stole my laptop?" Ned exclaimed, his eyes widening. "Are you serious?"

"I don't know if it was the Baxter campaign or someone else," I replied. "But one thing I *am* pretty sure of: This was not a random crime committed by someone who was just going for something of value."

Ned folded his arms. "How do you figure?"

I gestured around the room. "Look at this place. It's full of desks and computer equipment and tangles of cables on the floor. And your workstation is nowhere near the door. If someone was just looking to snatch something fast, they'd go for the stuff that's much more easily reachable. It would be way too easy to trip over something or someone in the dark and get caught."

There was another thing on my mind, but I didn't want to mention it to Ned just yet, because I knew it would upset him. The way I was thinking, there was a good possibility this was an inside job.

"Can you remember who was in the room and where they were when the lights went out?" I asked him.

Ned blew out his breath in a long sigh. "There were a lot of people here. Me, Richard, Gretchen, Mike, Tony, Cassandra." He waved his arm at three other volunteers, who were talking by the copier. "A couple of other people who'd just had a meeting with Richard—big-money campaign donors. Oh, and there was a courier delivering an envelope to Gretchen."

"The donors and the courier—did they leave?" I asked.

"Yeah, but don't get any ideas," Ned said. "I know how you think, Nancy, but it wasn't someone here. Richard made everyone stay in the room until the police arrived to take statements, and he also asked everyone to open their bags and briefcases to show my computer wasn't in there. He opened up his own briefcase first. He managed to get everyone to agree to it without upsetting anyone, even the donors. It was kind of amazing."

"I guess that's what makes him a good politician," I commented, glancing once again at Richard Solomon. He was leaning over Gretchen's shoulder, pointing to something on her computer screen and gesturing, his face intent.

He left the room, I thought. He went down to the basement to turn the lights back on. But why would Richard Solomon steal one of his own people's computers?

"Can I see the basement?" I asked Ned.

"I guess so," Ned agreed, looking mystified. "This way."

He led me through the hall to a metal door at the far end. I followed him down a flight of concrete steps into a basement that smelled of damp and mold. The whole thing was lit by one of those old-style fluorescent lights that flickered and hummed.

The circuit box was on the wall to the left of the stairs. I looked around it, but there was no place to hide a laptop. I poked around the shadowy corners of the big room, but found nothing. Also, judging by the level of grime on most of the surfaces, the place hadn't been touched in a long time. No, if Richard Solomon had brought Ned's laptop down here, he hadn't left it here. Of course, he could have had an accomplice—someone who had flipped the circuit breakers in the basement in the first place.

"Any idea what caused the blackout?" I asked Ned.

He shook his head. "No, but we did set up three more computers and a second printer yesterday. That's a big load for the circuits in an old building like this. It's not really surprising."

Now it was my turn to shrug. What I know about electrical circuits is basically nothing. Maybe it was just a random theft, I thought. Just more bad luck for poor Ned.

The idea hit me as we were walking back up the stairs. I stopped short, and Ned, who was behind me, bumped into me. "Whoa!" he said.

"Sorry," I said breathlessly. I walked up the last three steps. "It's just that I thought of something."

"What?" Ned put his hand on my arm.

"Well . . ." I was still working out the idea in my head as the words tumbled out of my mouth. "Yesterday your camera was stolen. Today your laptop was stolen. What do those two things have in common?"

"You mean besides the fact that they're both mine?" Ned said mournfully. Then he snapped his fingers. "Hey! They've both got photos stored on them!"

"Exactly!" I said. "Your camera is digital. And you usually download your photos on your computer and sort them before you burn them to a disc and get them developed, right?"

"Right. So you're thinking . . ." Ned trailed off, looking at me expectantly.

"I'm thinking," I said, facing him and putting my

hands on his shoulders, "that whoever burgled your house yesterday is the same person who stole your laptop today. And that person wasn't after your mother's bracelet at all. They were after your photos!"

7

Road Hazard

Whoa!" Ned said again. His brown eyes were wide. "Someone's after my photos?"

"I think so, although I don't know why—yet," I said. "Maybe you shot a picture of something you weren't supposed to see."

Ned exhaled slowly. "Well, that definitely puts a new spin on things."

"Yeah," I agreed. "There's one problem, though, and it's a big one."

"What do you mean?"

I sighed. "Well, now that whoever it is has the camera, and your laptop, they've got what they were after—and we don't know what that is. I don't suppose you got around to getting prints made of any of your photos?"

Ned's shoulders slumped. "No. I was going to burn a disc tonight, actually. I wanted to get the ones of Dad and the fish blown up and framed."

"What other pictures did you take?" I asked. "There can't be that many, right?" I added hopefully. "I mean, you just got the camera a couple of weeks ago. And digital cameras don't hold a lot of photos in their memory, do they?"

"Mine did," Ned assured me glumly. "I bought a memory card for it that tripled its capacity. I must have taken fifty or sixty shots over the last week. There were the fishing shots, of course, but there were also a bunch of pictures of last week's campaign rally in Littlefield and Richard's speech at the dedication of the new Solomon building at the university."

Campaign shots? Maybe Gretchen was right and the theft did have something to do with the campaign. Who else would want a bunch of photos of rallies?

Suddenly Ned grabbed my hand again. "Wait a second! I just thought of something. I e-mailed a bunch of those shots to Gretchen in case she wanted to use any of them for publicity. Maybe she still has them!"

My heart leaped. "Let's go see!"

Ned and I hurried back into the campaign office. Richard Solomon was still there, talking on his cell phone while scrolling through e-mails on one of the campaign computers. Gretchen and Mike were talking in low voices by the water cooler. Mike was scowling, I noticed.

"Gretchen," Ned said, crossing to her. "Do you remember those photos I e-mailed you on Sunday night?"

"You mean the rally shots?" Gretchen asked. "Sure. There were some really good ones in there. Why?"

"Do you still have them?" Ned asked. "I—"

"He just wanted to show me something," I said before he could explain further. Not that I seriously thought any of the Solomon people had anything to do with this case, but still, I didn't want to tip my hand, just in case.

"Yeah, I put them in the photo archive on the server," Gretchen said. "All the pictures are filed by date. You should be able to find them with no problem."

"Thanks!" Ned said, and hurried to a free computer. I pulled up a chair and sat beside him as he scrolled through the photo files.

"Here it is—Littlefield rally," he said after a moment. Clicking on the first of the photos, he opened it.

The angle of the shot showed that Ned had been standing in front of the speaker's podium. Richard Solomon stood there flanked by people I assumed were the town of Littlefield's important citizens. There was a woman with steel-gray hair and glasses, wearing a red suit, on his left, and a short man in a dark blue suit and tie on his right.

"That's Simon Keong, the mayor of Littlefield, and Letitia Allen, who's a big donor," Ned told me.

I scanned the other faces in the picture. No one stood out as looking particularly sneaky or out of place.

Ned clicked to the next shot. In this one and the next few after it, Richard Solomon was walking through the crowd, shaking hands right and left. Again, I looked carefully at the faces of the crowd, but everyone looked perfectly normal and happy. This is going to be tough, I thought. I have no idea what I'm even looking for!

I shook my head. "Maybe we should move on to the shots taken here in River Heights."

Richard Solomon had finished his phone call and wandered over to stand behind us. "What are you looking at?" he wanted to know.

"Just some shots of your campaign," I said cautiously. I didn't really think Solomon was likely to be involved in this . . . whatever it was, but like I said, I prefer to be careful when I'm not sure.

"Hah!" Solomon said with a smile. He leaned forward and pointed at a face on the computer screen.

"That is a great shot of Bill Snead. What a face that guy has! He looks like Abe Lincoln without the beard."

Snead? I knew that name. As I turned back to the screen I saw with surprise that the man shaking Richard Solomon's hand in front of the new Solomon building on the campus of the University of River Heights was none other than the marina manager I'd spoken to just that morning.

"You two know each other?" I asked.

"Oh, sure," Solomon said. "Bill and I used to work together, back when we were youngsters. I started on the floor at my father's paper plant, you know. Bill and I were on the same shift. We've gone down different paths since then, but I still try to keep up with him."

Ned clicked to the next shot. In that one, Solomon had his arm around an elderly woman who was beaming up at him. "That's Mrs. Crabtree. She was my civics teacher," he said. "She's the one who got me interested in public policy way back when. I kind of owe this campaign to her."

"I bet she's very proud of you," I commented.

Solomon shrugged and smiled. "She was a good teacher."

In the next shot, an intense-looking man with dark hair in a stringy ponytail was reaching over the shoulder of the woman in front of him, shaking a finger at Richard Solomon. "That guy was one of the ones asking about my paper plant's environmental track record," Solomon commented.

Gretchen had come up to look on, as well, and she snorted. "You know who that is? That's Raelene Baxter's campaign manager, Ralph Vaughn. He's the one I told you about. Watch out for him. There's nothing he won't do to win."

Ralph Vaughn. I made a mental note of the name.

"Well." Solomon stepped back and clapped his hands together. "Be that as it may, I don't see that there's much we can do about it right now. If the Baxter campaign really did shut off our power and steal Ned's computer, I'm sure it'll all come out sooner or later. In the meantime, I think we all deserve a little relaxation after a day like today. Come on, everyone, we're going out for Chinese. My treat. You, too, Nancy!"

"Oh, I don't want to intrude," I started to say, but he cut me off.

"Don't be silly. This isn't a working dinner, it's just fun. Please—join us."

"Well . . ." I knew that tonight was Hannah's night off, so I wouldn't be leaving her in the lurch. Besides, I couldn't turn down such a gracious invitation. And I could really go for some lo mien—my mouth was watering just thinking about it!

I quickly phoned Hannah to let her know what I was doing, then we all headed out to our cars. When Ned and I arrived at the restaurant, Solomon, Gretchen, and Mike were already seated and holding a table for seven. Tony and Cassandra, the other two volunteers, came in a moment after us. Soon we were all laughing and talking over sodas, and steaming dishes of stir-fry, noodles, and rice. All except Mike, who sat next to Gretchen looking sulky.

I ended up sitting between Ned and Richard Solomon, and we all fell into conversation.

"Did you really work on the floor at the paper mill?" I asked him.

"I sure did," he said, and laughed. "Why, don't you think I look strong enough?"

I felt my cheeks turn pink as I smiled. "It's not that," I said quickly. "You just seem like more of an office type."

"One thing my father insisted on was that I know the paper business from the ground up," Solomon told me. "Every summer while I was in college I worked at the mill, and after I graduated I went to work there full-time. I did everything from running the cutting machines to driving the logging trucks. It was great experience. It also showed me where our mill could be doing things more efficiently, with less damage to the environment."

"Solomon Paper was one of the first mills in the country to switch to chlorine-free papermaking, back in 1992," Ned told me.

"Also one of the first mills to switch to a closed-loop system, which means that all the water we use in our production process gets recycled and reused rather than pumped out into our waterways," Solomon said.

"And Solomon Paper's employees have the highest pay and best pension plan of any in the industry," Tony added.

"All of which is why Richard is the right person to be governor of our state," Gretchen chimed in from Solomon's other side. "He's a businessman who has proven that he can balance human needs with the big environmental issues we're facing and make it all work."

I noticed Mike rolling his eyes as Gretchen spoke.

I raised my eyebrows. "Well, I'm convinced. But what are you going to do about the Baxter campaign? They keep trying to blame Solomon Paper for the toxic chemicals in the river. Aren't you worried that people will believe them?"

"It's so ridiculous," Cassandra scoffed. "Especially since all the fish that were found with toxins in them came from upriver. Even if Solomon Paper *were* dumping pollutants into the river, they'd only show up in fish downstream from the plant."

"But we're not dumping," Richard Solomon said firmly, "and I intend to prove that beyond a shadow of a doubt. In fact, I've invited a team of environmental scientists to tour the plant this coming Friday. I guarantee they will find that we exceed all safety regulations by a large margin." He glanced at Ned. "Your dad is sending a reporter and a photographer along. I think the Baxter campaign will find this whole witch hunt leaves them looking worse than before."

"Wow," I said, impressed. Richard Solomon really did seem to have all the right ideas.

When I checked my watch I was surprised to see that it was already nine thirty. "Whoops," I said to Ned. "I've got to get going. I've got another early-morning jog tomorrow, and Bess and I have got to do better than we did this morning or George is going to go nuts."

"Leaving already, Nancy?" asked Solomon, who'd overheard me.

"Unfortunately, I have to," I told him, and explained about the 10-K race training.

"I think it's great that you're doing your part," he told me. "It's been a real pleasure talking to you. Now, if I could ask just one favor: I hope you'll leave Ned with us. I know I said this wasn't a working dinner, but I do need to talk a little campaign business with the team. Ned, I'm happy to give you a lift home if you can spare me another half hour or so."

"No problem," Ned said.

He walked me out to my car. "Working on this campaign has been intense, but really fun," he told me. "Richard is great, of course, but I like the campaign staff a lot too."

"You all seem to get along really well," I commented as I dug through my bag for my car keys. "The only one I didn't get much sense of is Mike." As far as I could tell, he hadn't said a single word during the entire dinner.

"Yeah, he's a dark horse," Ned agreed. "He's Gretchen's boyfriend, and I suspect he's only working on this campaign so he can keep an eye on her. He seems like the jealous type."

"Well, she is kind of gung-ho about Richard Solomon," I said cautiously. "Maybe Mike feels left out."

"Maybe." Ned shrugged. "So . . . it seems like your case is taking off in a whole new direction, huh?"

I finally found my keys and fished them out. They were tangled up in the cord of my iPod. As I unwound the wire, I said, "I feel like I'm on the right track now, but it's hard without knowing exactly what the criminal was after. I need to spend some more time looking through your photos. Do you think you could stop by the campaign office and e-mail them to me sometime tomorrow morning?"

"Sure thing," Ned promised. He kissed me good night and I drove off.

It had started to rain again while we were in the restaurant, and I flicked on the radio to see if I could get a weather report. "I really hope this clears up by tomorrow morning," I muttered. The last thing I needed was another adventure in the mud!

I hit the tuner button a few times as I drove, hunting for a weather report. Then I caught a few notes of one of my favorite songs, so I stopped the dial and sang along. Now, I can honestly say that there are many things I'm good at, but singing is not one of them. However, when I'm by myself there's nothing I like more than to just let it all out and pretend I can actually carry a tune.

I cranked up the volume and tapped my fingers on the steering wheel. "I know it's more than love, baby," I crooned. The windshield wipers were swishing in time with the beat as I navigated the curves of River Road. "When I'm close to you . . ."

Bright lights flashed in my rearview mirror and I squinted in annoyance. Whoever was behind me was tailgating me. "Turn your high-beams off!" I grumbled, as if the other driver could hear me.

Maybe he did hear, because the lights behind me shifted to my left. "I don't believe it!" I muttered. He was going to try to pass me! On the curviest part of the drive, in the rain! "What a jerk!"

As the other vehicle pulled alongside my little car, I glanced to my left and saw that it was a big, dark-colored SUV with tinted windows. I slowed down to let it get past me, but it didn't surge ahead. Instead, the truck matched my speed. What was the driver doing?

The truck began drifting to the right—into my lane.

My heart skipped a beat. I slammed my hand down on my horn. "Hey!" I yelled.

The truck kept coming.

"No way!" I gasped, as I realized what was happening.

The truck was trying to run me off the road!

8

Treading Water

Instinctively I hit the brakes. My tires screeched, then my car started to fishtail on the wet, curving road. My pulse was thundering as I eased up on the brake, then tapped it lightly. "Pump the brake and steer into the skid," I said aloud, the voice of my driver's ed teacher echoing in my mind.

Of course, my driver's ed teacher never told us what to do when someone in a big SUV was trying to shove us into a drainage ditch. . . .

I took my eyes off the road for a second to glance left again. The SUV was still there beside me, crowding my lane. My rearview mirror showed me that there were headlights behind me, so I couldn't just stop. And we were on the scenic stretch of River

Road—the part that ran along a bluff high above the river. There was no place to pull over.

What could I do? My hands on the steering wheel were wet with sweat. "Think, think!" I muttered to myself.

Then I saw the scariest sight of all: the headlights of a big truck coming toward us. Its horn blared an urgent warning, and its lights flashed on and off. My mind went blank. This is it, was all I could think.

The SUV's engine suddenly roared and it shot ahead of me. I hit the brakes again as it swerved into my lane. A shower of spray flew at my windshield. Then the SUV was accelerating away into the night, its taillights shrinking.

It was over!

Somehow I managed to keep driving until I could steer my car into the scenic pull-over spot a quarter of a mile ahead. I put the car in park and just sat there for a few minutes, trying to breathe. My whole body was shaking, and I felt cold all over.

Did that really just happen? Did someone really try to run me off the road?

Slowly my heartbeat stopped thudding against my ribs. And as I calmed down, I began to think again.

Maybe it wasn't what I had thought at first. If the driver of the SUV had really wanted to make me crash, he could have done it, I realized. His vehicle was so much larger than mine that it would have been no problem to push me right off the road. Instead, he had hovered beside me, crowding me without our cars actually ever touching.

"Maybe he was just trying to scare me," I said out loud. I held my hand out in front of me. It was still trembling. "Well, guess what? It worked!"

Finally I put my car into gear and drove the rest of the way home. But it was a long time before I could fall asleep.

When George and Bess came to pick me up the next morning, I was waiting on my porch.

"Nancy, you look awful!" Bess exclaimed when she saw my face. Then, realizing how that must have sounded, she added quickly, "I mean, you look pretty—you always do—but you also look like you didn't sleep a wink last night."

"That's because I didn't," I said as I fell into step beside my friends. "George, let's take it easy for a while. I need to tell you guys what's going on."

The three of us moved at a slow jog as I described the events of yesterday afternoon and evening, starting with the theft of Ned's laptop and ending with my terrifying adventure on River Road.

"I can't believe it!" Bess gasped.

"Do you think it was related to your new case?" George asked me.

I nodded. "It has to be. I spent a long time thinking about that while I was lying in bed last night. Here's what I figure." I paused and took a swig of water.

"It seems to me that someone in the Solomon campaign has to be behind everything," I went on. "It's the only explanation that covers all the bases. I mean, Ned's camera was stolen Monday, his laptop the next day. Both had pictures from the campaign on them. Then I showed up at the campaign office and announced that I'm a detective and I'm going to investigate. Just a few hours later someone was trying to scare me off. The only people who even knew about my investigation were the people who were in that office and at that dinner last night. It has to be one of them."

"But didn't you say they were all still there when you left the restaurant?" George asked.

"That's true," I said. "But I called Ned when I got home last night and he told me Gretchen's boyfriend, Mike, left a few minutes after me. He said he thought Mike and Gretchen had had some kind of fight."

We turned right onto Morrow Drive, a quiet, tree-lined road that led to a park with a running trail. "Can we slow down?" Bess asked plaintively. "I don't have . . . enough breath . . . to ask all the questions I want to ask."

"We're already basically walking," George grumbled. But she slowed the pace a little more. To my surprise, I was enjoying this morning's run. Maybe because we were taking an easier pace, or maybe because I actually do better on no sleep—whatever the reason, I felt full of energy.

"So you think this guy Mike is . . . like, a double agent . . . for the Baxter campaign?" Bess asked after we'd jogged in silence for a moment.

"That's what I'm wondering," I replied. "The problem is, I can't figure out how to find out more. I feel like an idiot for not trying to get at least a glimpse at the license plate on that SUV last night. If I had the numbers I could ask Officer Johansen to look it up for me on the police database and see if it's registered to Mike."

"Well," George pointed out, "it was dark and raining. Plus you were kind of busy trying to keep from, you know, crashing."

"I guess so," I said with a grin. George could be good at putting things in perspective for me.

"If you know what kind of car it is . . . and you know . . . Mike's full name . . . can Officer Johansen look up . . . the registration that way?" Bess panted.

"I guess she could," I said. "But I have no idea what kind of car it was. You know me, Bess, I don't pay attention to those kind of things. All I know is that it was a big SUV. And it had a panel on the side that was a lighter color."

"Well, that's something!" Bess said. "Can you remember . . . anything else about it? Did you . . . happen to notice . . . the shape of the grille or the . . . headlights? How about the . . . wheel wells?"

I gave her a sidelong look. Bess may seem like the girliest girl you could ever imagine, but she happens to be a whiz at anything mechanical. And she loves cars. She's the only person I know who subscribes to both *Glamour* and *Car and Driver*.

"Well," I said, wrinkling my brow as I tried to picture the SUV, "I don't think I saw the grille. When it was behind me, the headlights were so bright that I couldn't see any details. But the thing was huge. It was twice as long as my car. And it was really square. Square hood, square body, square wheel wells." I snapped my fingers as I remembered something else. "And there was a little symbol on the back. Kind of a cross shape, I think."

"That clinches it!" Bess panted. "It's a Chevy . . . Suburban."

"You know that from what I just described?" I exclaimed. "Come on, I don't believe you."

"Believe me," Bess said. Slowing to a walk, she added, "There's more, but I cannot talk and run at the same time."

"Okay, stretching break," George declared.

We were at the park by now, so the three of us moved onto the grass. "Ow," Bess moaned, sprawling on her back. "I'm too sore to stretch."

"You really should," George told her. "Not stretching is one of the key causes of runners' injuries."

"Yeah, yeah," Bess grumbled. She sat up abruptly. "Ugh! This grass is soaking wet!"

"It rained last night, remember?" George said without much sympathy. Bracing her hands against a tree trunk, she began to stretch her calves.

I held out my hand to haul Bess to her feet. "What else did you figure out about the mystery SUV?" I asked as I settled into a lunge to stretch my hamstrings.

"Well, it has to be a Chevy, judging from the logo on the hatch. And it has to be a Suburban, because they're the biggest SUV around. Now, Chevy stopped putting the contrasting panels on the Suburban line several years ago," Bess said. "So the one that tried to squash you must be from the nineties. And if it's really as square as you say, it's probably from the early nineties. The Suburban got more streamlined after that."

"Bess, you're amazing!" I declared. "I can't believe you figured that all out from me saying it was big and square."

Bess smiled. "It's a gift."

"I'd better get home," I said. "I've got to make some phone calls!"

"I'll go with you," Bess said quickly. "You might need more help figuring out the car make."

"Nice try, you two," George said with a grin. "But it's not even seven in the morning yet. It's too early to make any phone calls, and we've still got another two miles to run."

As I realized she was right, I started to laugh. "I wasn't thinking," I said. "Sorry."

"Let's get going again," George said, starting to jog in place.

"Do we have to?" Bess whined.

"Deirdre Shannon," George reminded her.

"I'm not sure revenge is worth all this pain," Bess muttered as she started down the running path. "I'm really not!"

"You look even more tired than I feel," I told Ned.

He sighed. "I stayed up past three this morning, trying to reconstruct my Victorian poetry paper—the one that was on my laptop. Then I had a nine o'clock class. Then I went to the library to work on the paper some more. I'm going back after my two o'clock class too. This is the only break I'm taking all day."

"Sorry it's not more of a break," I said, taking his

hand. "Probably the last thing you want to do right now is stare at a computer screen."

"It's worth it if I can help you crack this case," he replied.

I'd spent the morning making phone calls. First I'd called Ned and gotten the full names of Mike and all the other campaign workers. I figured I might as well check them all out. Then I'd called my friend Ellen Johansen at the River Heights PD.

"I need a favor," I told her. "Can you check these names and find out what kind of cars they own? I'm looking for an old Chevy Suburban."

"No problem, Nancy," she said. "But it's going to take me a little while. I'm just heading over to the courthouse to testify in a traffic violation case. Can I get back to you later this afternoon?"

"Whatever you can do would be great," I said. "Thanks, Ellen. I owe you one."

"Hah! The River Heights PD owes you about fifty," she said with a laugh. "I just need to be discreet. You know Chief McGinnis gets bent out of shape when I do you any favors."

"I know," I had replied. "Don't worry, my lips are sealed."

Now it was lunchtime and Ned and I had met at Solomon campaign headquarters once again, so that we could check the photo archives to see if anything jumped out at us as suspicious or strange. What photo could Ned have taken that would drive someone to steal both his camera and his laptop?

Grasping the mouse, Ned clicked it and a new photo popped up on the screen. He stared at it for a moment, then shook his head.

"Sorry, but I don't even know these people," he said. "It's just a crowd shot. And I think this is the last one I took." He clicked the mouse again and the first picture we'd looked at popped up again. "Yep, that was the last one. I remember I had to leave before the end of the dedication ceremony because it was Tuesday and I had an economics class."

"Tuesday?" I repeated. "This ceremony was last Tuesday?"

"Yeah," Ned said, turning in his seat to look questioningly at me. "Why?"

"What day was the rally in Littlefield?" I asked, frowning.

"The day before—Monday." Ned raised his eyebrows. "What about it?"

I tapped my fingers on the desk. "It just isn't really adding up," I said slowly. "If you took these photos last Monday and Tuesday, that means they were available for a full week before the thefts happened. Why would the person who stole your stuff wait so long?"

"I don't know," Ned said. "Maybe whoever it was didn't know they existed until now. After all, I didn't e-mail them to Gretchen until Sunday night. That was the first time anyone but me saw them." He snapped his fingers. "And if it was Mike who did it, like you suggested, then that makes sense. Gretchen probably showed them to him and that's when he got the idea to steal my stuff."

"Except that he didn't delete the copies of the photos that are right here on the server where everyone can see them," I pointed out. "Even though that would have been totally easy for him to do."

"Oh, right," Ned said. He leaned back in his chair and rubbed his face wearily. "Come to think of it, anyone working on the campaign could easily have deleted the photos from the archive, but no one did. I'm confused. Does that mean we're not looking at someone from the campaign after all?"

"I don't know what it means," I said, frustrated. "It seems to me that it has to be someone from the campaign. But maybe we're missing something else. Try to remember, Ned. Were there any other photos on your camera or your computer besides the ones in the archive?"

"Just the ones of my fishing trip with Dad," Ned said. "I'm sure of that."

"Is it possible there was something in one of those photos that someone wanted to keep secret?" I wondered aloud.

Ned shook his head. "I can't imagine what. Or who would even know I took them, besides me, my Dad, and Lonny."

"Lonny again," I murmured. Maybe I shouldn't have written him off as a suspect so quickly. . . .

My cell phone rang and I fished it out of my bag. It was Ellen Johansen.

"No luck," she said as soon as I'd greeted her. "None of the names you gave me drive a Chevy Suburban or anything close, I'm afraid. Mike Duffy rides a motorcycle, Gretchen Hochman drives a Toyota sedan, Tony Buteo drives a Jeep, Cassandra Colon drives a Honda sedan, and Richard Solomon drives a Lexus hybrid."

"Okay, thanks," I told her. "At least that tells me I need to keep looking for clues."

I flipped the phone closed and sat there for a moment, staring into space. The clues I had were a stolen camera, a stolen laptop, and a car that had tried to run me off the road. But there was nothing that linked them all together.

There must be something I was missing, something that would cause this crazy case to suddenly make sense. But I had no idea what it was.

"I'm stuck," I said aloud.

How in the world was I going to solve this mystery?

9

Breaking the Surface

N ancy," Ned said. Then a little louder: "Earth to Nancy. Come in!"

I gave myself a little shake. "Sorry. Just thinking . . ."

"Got any bright ideas?" Ned asked me.

I sighed and stood up, stretching. "Not really. At this point, the only thing I can think of is that maybe you and I should take a boat and go fishing."

"Huh?" Ned wrinkled his forehead.

"It's sort of a desperation move," I admitted. "But it's possible that we've been focusing on the wrong photos. Maybe the picture you took that someone is so worried about was actually taken during your fishing trip."

"The timing makes more sense, doesn't it," Ned said thoughtfully. "My camera was stolen the next day, and the computer the day after that."

"Right. Not much else about it makes sense, but it's a place to start," I said. "So I figure, maybe if you and I get a boat and go back out there, we'll be able to get some idea of what the mystery picture is."

"Sounds like a plan," Ned said. He stood up. "Can it wait until four thirty this afternoon? I've got a class that I'd really hate to miss."

I shrugged. "I guess so. George wants to start collecting pledges for our run, so I've got plenty to keep me busy."

"Okay, then." Ned put his arm around my shoulders and gave me a quick squeeze. "Pick me up at the university at four thirty?"

"It's a date," I agreed.

I drove home, where Bess and George met me for one of Hannah's delicious lunches of soup, salad, and homemade rolls. Then George and I hit the pavement, asking people to pledge a donation if we completed the charity race. Bess was supposed to come with us, but she begged off at the last minute because her mom had asked her to stay home and wait for a furniture delivery. "I'm sorry, guys!" she said. "I promise I'll do double duty tomorrow." As she stood up, she winced. "To tell you the truth, I don't know how much pounding of the pavement I'd be able to do, anyway. My legs are a little sore after this morning's workout."

"You'd better stretch when you get home," George warned. "If you don't, you'll be even more sore tomorrow."

"Don't worry about me," Bess said airily. "I'll just take a hot bath tonight."

"And stretch!" George called after her. Bess just waved without turning around.

"Shall we?" I said to George, picking up my clipboard and pledge forms.

"We shall," she agreed, and we headed out.

"We're doing really well!" George said after a couple of hours. "We got twenty-six pledges. Not bad for our first day."

"Not bad at all," I agreed.

"We are so going to flatten Deirdre Shannon," Bess said gleefully when we called her to give her the update. I put her on speaker so George could join in.

"Did you stretch yet?" George wanted to know.

"What are you, my mother? I was just about to!" Bess said.

"Do it," George advised.

"Bye, Bess," I said, and hung up.

Checking my watch, I saw that I still had almost an hour before I had to meet Ned. "Come on. Let's go to Mugged and celebrate our pledges with mocha lattes."

As we walked in, I spotted a familiar head of curly black hair at the cashier's stand. Deirdre Shannon— our competition, and Bess's nemesis.

"Oh, hello," she said when we greeted her. She looked us both up and down with her usual expression of faint disgust. "If you're hoping to get Mugged to pledge you for the race, forget it. I already got them to promise they'd pledge me and nobody else."

I could see George gritting her teeth to keep from snapping out a retort. "Well," I said pleasantly, "I don't know if getting people to agree NOT to give to charity is really the right way to do it, but that's okay. I'm sure we can find plenty of people to pledge our team."

"My father had his secretary send out pledge forms to all his clients at the law firm," Deirdre said. "I'm going to win this."

I kept my smile with difficulty. "As long as the money is going to help the environment, it's all good, right?" Our coffees arrived and we carried them to a table.

"See you later, DeeDee," George called over her shoulder, and chuckled as we heard Deirdre huff with annoyance. She hates being called DeeDee, which is why George can't resist calling her that.

"Wow. Have you ever met anyone more irritating?" George said in an undertone.

"You know, I really don't think I have," I replied, shaking my head. "She is amazing."

"You didn't seem to be bothered by her snarky comments," George told me.

"Believe me, it was an act." I sipped my latte. "She annoyed me plenty. I didn't really care about beating Deirdre before, but I do now. We have got to get more pledges than she does."

George grinned. "That's the spirit!"

I sighed. "But first I've got to solve this case. Which gets more baffling by the hour. Each time I think I know what's going on, it turns out I'm on the wrong track."

"You'll get it," George told me. "You always do."

"I hope you're right," I murmured.

After we finished our coffees I dropped George back at her house. Then I picked Ned up and we drove to the marina. As we pulled into a parking space in the muddy unpaved lot I was struck by how run-down the place looked. Today there were only four boats in the slips, and one of those was a sailboat that appeared to be half-wrecked. The old fishing trawler was still tied up at the far dock, and two battered aluminum power boats bobbed in the water by the fuel pumps. There was no one in sight.

"My dad says this place is going to be shut down at the end of the season," Ned remarked, as if reading my thoughts. "A national chain of boatyards has bought the land and is planning to demolish this old marina and build a new one, with a fancy restaurant and all new boating facilities. They figure the people who buy those new riverfront condos that are going up by the golf course will want a bigger, better, more modern place to keep their boats."

"It makes me a little sad," I admitted as we walked toward the office. "I mean, I guess it's progress, but still, there's something kind of cool about old places like this."

"Yeah. They have a lot of history," Ned agreed.

"I wonder what's going to happen to Lonny and Mr. Snead?" I said.

"I guess they'll have to find other work," Ned said, shrugging.

A battered motorcycle was parked in front of the marina office, and when we went in, we found Lonny seated behind the counter, engrossed in a handheld video game. When I cleared my throat, he jumped and looked up.

"Whoa! You two scared me. First people I've seen all day," he told us. His forehead wrinkled as he recognized me. "Hey, you never sent me your e-mail address. Or your friend's," he said reproachfully.

"Sorry," I said. "I just haven't gotten around to it yet. I will."

"Heard that before," he said in a gloomy undertone. "Anyway, what can I do for you?"

"We'd like to rent a motorboat," Ned said.

"Now?" Lonny eyed us doubtfully. "It's going to be dark soon. We don't allow boating after dark— there are no running lights on the boats. Why don't you come back tomorrow?"

"We promise we'll be back before dark," I said quickly. "We just want to go out on the river for a little while. Please?"

"Well, I don't know. Mr. Snead would be mad," he said. "He's always worried about bringing the law down on this place."

"We won't bring the law down on the marina," Ned said. I could tell from his voice that he was trying not to laugh.

"Okay," Lonny finally gave in. "But be sure you're back here by five thirty. That's when I close up. And don't tell Mr. Snead."

"Promise," I said. "Thanks, Lonny."

He handed us two orange life preservers and a padlock key. "Take the one on the left," he instructed. "The other one doesn't have any gas."

We used the key to unchain the boat from the dock. Then Ned started it up and I climbed into the bow. I pushed aside a set of wooden oars that were resting on the plank seat and settled myself in. Then Ned guided us away from the dock and out into the current.

"So where were you fishing?" I asked, speaking loudly to be heard over the putt-putt of the outboard motor.

Ned pointed to a spot about a hundred yards downriver, right where the golf course ended. There was a creek that fed into the river at that point, creating a small bay with a rock-strewn bank.

"Isn't that the site where the new condos are supposed to go?" I asked. "There, on the far side of the golf course?"

"I think so," Ned said. He steered the little boat toward the bay. "I heard they're going to call the development Half Moon Bay."

"That sounds romantic," I said. "But it kind of makes me think of pirates."

"I know what you mean," Ned agreed, laughing.

As we came nearer, he slowed the engine to barely more than a stutter. "I think we dropped the anchor right about . . . here," he said.

"Okay," I said. "Now, think back. Try to reconstruct exactly what you saw while you were fishing."

Ned screwed up his face as he tried to recall. "I was sitting in the stern, like I am now," he said. "I was facing upriver and toward the bank. The sun was just coming up, I remember, because it was sparkling so brightly on the water that I could barely see." He shifted in his seat. "Hey! There were a couple of golfers onshore. I remember thinking they must be dedicated—it was awfully early to be golfing on a Sunday morning."

"Okay," I encouraged him. "How do you know they were golfers? Were they carrying clubs?"

"They were carrying some kind of long, skinny things," Ned said. "I assumed they were clubs, but with the sun in my eyes, I really couldn't make out any details." He frowned. "You know, as I picture it in my mind, I'm realizing that they might not have been golfers after all. They were standing on the far side of the stream—past the edge of the golf course." He pointed toward the shore.

Excitement stirred inside me. "Good," I said. "That's great! Can you take us in to shore? I'd like to have a look around at the spot where you think they were."

"You got it." Twisting the throttle, Ned cranked up the outboard motor and steered the boat in. Soon we were climbing ashore at a spot between two big boulders. I helped Ned drag the boat a little ways up onto the bank so it wouldn't float away.

"Ugh! It's super muddy here," I said as my foot slid

sideways on the rain-softened ground. "Be careful."

We picked our way up the slope to a spot about fifteen yards from the little creek. "The guys I saw were standing right about here," Ned told me.

I gazed around. My heart thudded as I spotted a mound of fresh earth. The recent rain had flattened it out, but it was still obvious that someone had been digging here quite recently.

"Those long things you saw in the men's hands— do you think they could have been shovels?" I asked.

"I guess they could have been," Ned said, shrugging. "But so what? It's a construction site. It makes sense that people would be digging here."

"Construction on the condos hasn't started yet," I said. "I happen to know that the developers are still waiting for their final permits. One of the lawyers in my dad's firm is handling it for them. And, anyway, even if it had started, how many construction workers do you know who come out at sunrise on a Sunday morning?"

The small hairs on the back of my neck prickled. My intuition was shouting at me that, at last, we'd found something that might be important.

"Come on," I said, and plunged back down the slippery hill to the shore.

"What are you doing?" Ned asked as I fished the oars out of the bottom of the boat.

I handed him one. "We'll have to use these. We don't have time to go back and get shovels."

"Shovels?" he repeated. "You mean we're going to dig?"

"That's right," I said, and started back to the mound of dirt. "I want to see what those men were burying."

I reached the site and started scraping at the water-logged soil with the blade of the oar. In a moment Ned was at my side, doing the same thing. We worked fast and in silence. The only thing I could hear was my heartbeat pounding in my ears.

What would we discover buried in the ground?

I was almost afraid to find out. . . .

10

Diving In

It was Ned who said what I was trying not to think.

"Nancy, you don't think there's a . . . well, a body buried here, do you?" he asked in a hushed voice.

I licked my lips nervously. "I have no idea," I said. "I really hope not. But honestly, I don't know what we're going to find."

We scraped away for another minute or two. Then Ned wrinkled his nose. "Do you smell something?"

I sniffed. "No," I told him. Then a faint whiff of something hit me. It was unpleasantly sharp and sweet at the same time. And familiar, though for the moment I couldn't place it. "Ugh. Yes, I do!"

An instant later I felt the soil give way under my makeshift shovel. I lost my balance and stumbled forward into the shallow hole we'd dug. As I hit its bottom, the ground gave way under me and I fell about three feet straight down, in a shower of mud and small rocks. "Help!" I wailed.

"Nancy!" Ned cried, crouching and holding out his hands to me. "Are you okay?"

"I think so," I said, catching my breath. "Just muddy. Again." I started to reach for his hand, then drew back. I'd just noticed that the pit I was standing in had strangely smooth sides. "Wait a second." Bending down, I peered more closely at an exposed earth wall of the hole. It stretched in a smooth curve, with small ridges running vertically across it about a foot apart. I poked at it with a finger. The dirt was hard packed, almost like cement. And there were odd streaks of red in the pale, yellowish clay.

"What's going on?" Ned asked.

"I'm not sure," I replied slowly. "But I think something was recently dug up here."

"You mean the people who were digging here weren't putting something in the ground, they were taking something out?" Ned asked. "Like . . . like buried treasure or something?"

"I don't know what," I said. "From the shape of the marks in the soil, it looks like it was some kind of big barrel." I scanned the area that had been dug up and added, "Maybe more than one. And it had been here long enough that it started to rust. See here, where the rust has stained the dirt?" I pointed at the reddish streaks.

"Let me have a look," Ned said. Dropping lightly down into the pit beside me, he crouched and studied the soil. "I see what you mean," he said after a moment. "The marks are in the shape of one of those big metal drums, like the kind they store oil or toxic chemicals in."

"Toxic chemicals?" I repeated. An alarm suddenly went off in my mind. "Oh, no! Ned, get out of this pit. Quick!" I gasped.

Without stopping to ask why, he scrambled up the side and reached down to haul me out. Only when we were both standing well back from the hole did he say, "What are you thinking, Nan?"

"The smell. The barrels. I know what was buried in here," I said breathlessly. "Toxic waste!"

"What?" He stared at me.

"This is it!" I declared. "It has to be! It's the source of the river pollution; it's the source of the awful smell that Bess and George and I noticed yesterday and you noticed today. It must have leaked!"

"What must have leaked?" Ned was looking confused.

"One of the barrels. It must have rusted through and the stuff inside must have seeped out into the ground." I drew a deep breath. "Ned, there were barrels of some kind of toxic waste buried here until recently—until Sunday morning at dawn, in fact. And I'm willing to bet that the reason your camera and computer were stolen is because when you took those pictures of your dad on Sunday morning, you also happened to take pictures of whoever was digging up the waste."

Ned's mouth hung open in astonishment for a moment. Then he snapped it shut and whistled. "Wow!" he said. "That's insane, Nancy. Why would someone dig up a bunch of toxic waste barrels?"

"I'm not totally sure," I admitted. I paced up and down, biting my lip as I tried to think it through. "I mean, I can figure out some of it. Clearly, whoever dug it up is the same person or people who put it here in the first place. They must have realized that with the condo construction due to start any day, the barrels would be uncovered soon, anyway. And they were afraid that somehow it would be traced back to them."

"So they came out here in the middle of the night to dig it up and move it," Ned said. He whistled again. "It's crazy, but it does all fit."

"Doesn't it?" I agreed. I shivered. "It's horrible. I can hardly believe someone would do something so awful right here in River Heights."

"I wonder who it was," Ned said.

"That's what I have to figure out," I said grimly. "Who moved it, where it came from, and most important, where it is now."

"Whoa, that's right!" Ned exclaimed. "Wherever it is, it's a hazard that has to be taken care of!"

I hunted through my bag until I found a small plastic Baggie. I usually carry a few of these with me just in case I need to collect evidence. Kneeling at the edge of the hole, I took a stick and gingerly scraped some of the soil into the Baggie. Sealing it, I put it back in my bag.

"Hey, Nan," Ned said suddenly. "We've got to get back to the marina pronto. It's got to be way past five thirty. The sun's almost down. Lonny is probably going nuts."

"Whoops! You're right." I grabbed the oars and we hurried back to the boat. Ned started up the engine, and five minutes later we were bumping up against the dock at the marina. I tossed Lonny the rope to tie us up and he gave me a reproachful glare.

"I'm so sorry we're late," I said sincerely. "We got kind of caught up in something."

"It's just lucky Mr. Snead didn't come back," Lonny grumbled. "He's almost always here, and boy, would he have been peeved."

"It is lucky," I agreed. "Sorry again, Lonny. We'll get out of your hair now."

Ned and I hurried to the car. "I don't know how much I'll be able to concentrate on my English paper, what with thinking about what we just found out," he said as we drove toward the university. "I guess it's a good thing I'm reconstructing it, rather than figuring out the whole thing from scratch. What are you going to do?"

I'd been considering that question. "I need to find a science lab," I said. "If I can find out what kind of pollutants are in that soil sample I took, maybe that'll help me figure out where it came from—and who dumped it."

By now it was almost seven in the evening. I dropped Ned off at the university, then found an Internet café nearby. After a few minutes of searching, I had phone numbers for five environmental science labs in the area. Three of them were at the University of River Heights, so I figured I'd try those first.

But before anything, I had to call Hannah.

"Don't tell me, let me guess," she said when she answered the phone. "You won't be home for supper tonight."

"I'm sorry, Hannah," I said. "You know I'd be there if I could. It's just that I think I'm close to cracking this case."

"Oh, all right. I don't suppose it can wait until morning," Hannah said with a sigh. "Well, I made a roast chicken. I'll put a plate in the oven for when you get home. And, Nancy?"

"Yes?"

"You be careful, you hear me?"

I smiled at the phone. "I hear you," I said. "'Night, Hannah. Don't wait up. And thanks."

I got lucky on my second phone call. Dr. Andrew Crippen happened to be working late at the university that evening. I arranged to meet him in his office in the science center.

Dr. Crippen was a thin, stooped man in his late forties with glasses and a reddish beard. "Let's have a look at what you've got," he said when I arrived.

I handed him the Baggie full of soil. When he unsealed it, the smell of burned cabbage and stinky socks wafted into the lab. "Whew," he said, wincing.

He pulled on a pair of rubber gloves. "The immuno-assay, which is the most definitive test we do for soil toxins, takes time. First I have to dry the sample overnight," he explained, emptying a small amount of soil from the Baggie onto a paper towel. He laid another paper towel onto it and then put the whole thing in a contraption that looked kind of like a fish tank. "Then it needs to be shaken in an agitator for at least two to four hours. Then I put it in a centrifuge and spin it to separate the components. And *then* we start the actual chemical testing. We have a new test that can be completed within twenty-four hours—the old one took at least five days—but you have to understand that I can't just work some lab magic right here and now and tell you with certainty what this stuff is."

"I see," I said, swallowing my impatience. "Well, do you have any guesses?"

He raised his eyebrows. "As a matter of fact, I do." Selecting an instrument that looked like a glass spoon with a tiny bowl, he scooped out a bit more of the soil and dumped it into a test tube. He poured some clear liquid from a beaker into the tube. "This is distilled water," he told me.

"Okay," I said, mystified.

Using a long pair of tweezers, Dr. Crippen selected a strip of blue litmus paper from a drawer and dipped it into the tube. Within a few seconds, the strip of paper began to turn white.

Dr. Crippen glanced up at me with a serious expression. "This tells me that there's a high concentration of chlorine in the test tube," he explained. "And I know the chlorine is from your sample, not from the water I added, because that water is distilled and contains no impurities."

"Is chlorine a problem?" I asked. "I thought it was a disinfectant."

"In very weak concentrations, yes. But pure chlorine is highly toxic," Dr. Crippen said. "For example, chlorine gas was used as a weapon in World War One, and its effects were so terrible that its use was outlawed by the Geneva convention in 1925. What's more, one of the by-products of chlorine is dioxin, which is known to cause cancer and a range of other diseases."

I felt a chill. "And that's in the sample I brought you?"

Dr. Crippen took off his glasses and polished them on his white lab coat. "Well, as I said, the only thing I know for sure right now is that there's chlorine in the soil, in levels that can't be accounted for naturally," he replied. "The tests that will tell us for certain exactly what's in the sample won't be completed before tomorrow afternoon. But the chlorine test tells me that my first suspicion is most likely correct."

"What was your first suspicion?" I asked.

"I worked for the Environmental Protection Agency several years ago," Dr. Crippen told me. "One of my tasks was to travel to industrial brownfields—that's what we call the sites where manufacturers used to bury their waste products—and figure out what was needed to clean them up. I visited many brownfields that had been created by paper mills, and I became very familiar with the characteristic odor of the sludge that used to be produced in the paper-making process. That's what this sample smells like.

I believe we'll learn that the soil is contaminated by toxic papermaking sludge."

I couldn't stifle a gasp. Papermaking sludge?

There was only one paper mill in River Heights. Solomon Paper.

And that meant that, more than likely, the person who was behind all the attempts to cover up this toxic waste problem was Richard Solomon.

A New Can of Worms

The odd thing is," Dr. Crippen said, shaking his head, "I happen to know that Solomon Paper hasn't used these compounds for years and years. I was one of the consultants who advised them on how to switch over to more environmentally friendly processes. I've been to the plant and I've studied its operation thoroughly. I don't think this could have come from there, but I can't think of any other likely source in the area."

I didn't reply. I was thinking about the rust marks Ned and I had seen in the dirt. Obviously, the barrels had been buried for many years. Maybe they were put there before Richard Solomon's time, I thought, and for a moment, I felt a spark of hope.

But then I thought of the car that had nearly run me off the road, and the spark went out. Richard

Solomon must have arranged that somehow. The timing—right after he found out that I was poking around into the thefts—was too perfect for it to be a coincidence.

With a start, I realized that Dr. Crippen had just asked me a question. "I'm sorry—what did you say?" I murmured.

"I said, if you give me a call here at the lab late tomorrow afternoon, I should have some definite answers for you," Dr. Crippen repeated.

"Right," I said. "That's great. Thanks for all your help, Dr. Crippen."

My thoughts churning, I walked out to my car. Richard Solomon, a criminal? I hated to believe it. I had come away from last night's dinner really admiring him.

And how was Ned going to react? Solomon was almost a hero to him! He would be devastated.

But on the other hand, if Richard Solomon did have something to do with those barrels of toxic waste, then obviously he was completely the wrong person to be governor. Anyone who would commit a crime like that deserved to go to jail.

Oh, this was hard!

And how on earth could I prove any of it?

Fishing out my cell phone, I called Bess. "Can I come over?" I asked when she answered the phone.

"I have a problem, and I need to talk it through."

"As long as you don't need me to move my body at all," Bess said. She groaned. "Ow! I think I may be permanently paralyzed from this morning."

"Did you stretch, like George told you to?" I demanded. "Bess, if you don't stretch after a workout, you're asking for trouble!"

"Don't yell at me," Bess begged. "I already got an earful from George. Listen, if you want to come over and talk, I'm here. But please don't lecture me. I'm already in enough pain."

"On my way," I said, and hung up.

Ten minutes later I pulled into Bess's driveway and parked behind her car. I greeted her parents and her little sister, Maggie, who were gathered in the living room watching TV. Then I headed up to Bess's room.

"Come in," she called when I knocked.

The poor thing was lying on her bed with heating pads draped over both legs. "They don't hurt as long as I don't move at all, or let anything touch them," she said.

"Did you take that hot bath?" I asked.

"By the time I remembered, I was too sore to walk to the bathroom," Bess told me. "But come on, Nancy. I don't want to talk about this. What did you want to discuss with me?"

I heaved a deep sigh as I sat down on the end of her bed. I told her about the signs of digging Ned and I had found, and my conclusion that toxic waste had been buried there. Then I told her what Dr. Crippen had said. "He thinks the toxic waste is paper sludge. If that's the case, it seems like Richard Solomon must be involved somehow," I said. "Which makes it a whole lot easier to explain things like the theft of Ned's laptop from campaign headquarters, and the attack on me that happened right after Solomon found out I was a detective."

"Wait a minute. Back up. Are you telling me that Richard Solomon broke into Ned's house and knocked out Ned's mother?" Bess demanded, her blue eyes round with disbelief.

"No, no." I waved my hands. "I'm not saying he did all this stuff himself. I'm pretty sure he has someone working with him. Or for him. Someone who does the dirty work for him. A henchman, I guess you could call it. Remember, Ned saw two people out there the morning of his fishing trip." My eyes narrowed as I thought. "In fact, if I could figure out who the henchman is, that would probably help me nail Solomon." Then I remembered my other problem and sighed again. "But I still don't know how on earth I'm going to break the news to Ned."

"It's going to hurt," Bess said gently. "But Ned's a

big boy, Nan. And I'm sure he'd rather find out now, before the election, rather than once Richard Solomon is governor."

"You're right," I said, picking at her pink bedspread with my fingernail. "I know you are. But I still feel sick about it."

"Well, let's focus on the other stuff," Bess suggested. "What else do we know? You said you thought the toxic waste had been buried a while, since there were rust marks in the dirt. How long ago do you think it was?"

"Good question," I said, perking up. I thought back to the things Solomon had told me about his paper plant at dinner the night before. "We know the plant switched to chlorine-free bleaches in 1992, so it was probably no later than that. And we know Solomon didn't start working in the plant until he was in college, so that gives us a likely place to start. Do you mind if I use your computer? I want to look up a few things."

"Be my guest," Bess said with a wave of her hand. "As long as you don't need me to move."

I sat down at her desk and logged on to the Internet. In a couple of minutes I was browsing the Solomon campaign's website, reading about his early career.

"It says here that he took over from his father in

1991, when he was twenty-eight, and immediately began converting the mill to chlorine-free bleach," I said. "If he started college when he was eighteen, that means he worked at the mill for at least ten years while they were still using chlorine bleach. And therefore, that stuff was probably buried right next to our river anywhere from fifteen to twenty-five years ago."

"Unbelievable," Bess muttered. "That poison has been there all this time!"

I leaned back in the desk chair and wearily ran my fingers through my hair. "I wonder how they knew Ned was the one taking pictures in the first place?" I mused. "I don't think he was close enough to shore for them to be able to see clearly who he was."

"Maybe they asked at the marina," Bess suggested. "After all, there couldn't have been too many people taking boats out at that hour on a Sunday morning. It probably wouldn't have been hard to get Ned's name from Lonny or that manager guy, Bill Snead."

Snead. I sat up straight as I suddenly remembered. "Bess!" I exclaimed. "Snead! Richard Solomon knows him! In fact, he told me they used to work together at the paper mill!"

Bess gasped. "You think Snead is the henchman?"

"It fits!" Jumping up, I began to pace around the room. "It fits perfectly. They were coworkers . . . for some reason they buried some barrels of waste from the paper plant in some unused land by the river . . . and then years later, it's about to be discovered, so they have to move it." I slapped a hand to my forehead as something else hit me. "Oh, I don't believe it. Bess, *I'm* the one who tipped Snead off that Ned had copies of the pictures on his computer. When I told him I was looking for Lonny, he wanted to know why, and I told him this dumb story about how I'd seen Ned's photos on his computer and I wanted to get a cell phone case like the one Lonny had. It was totally made up—I was just trying to come up with a reason that I had to talk to Lonny. But that very afternoon is when Ned's computer was stolen. Snead must have told Solomon and they planned it on the spot."

Bess's eyes were round. "This is huge, Nancy!" she said. "If you're right, it will totally kill Solomon's campaign!"

"Kill his campaign?" I said. "He'll go to jail—if I can prove any of it."

"But how?" Bess asked. "Without the photos Ned took, you don't have any evidence, do you?"

"Not unless I can find the barrels of toxic waste they dug up," I said.

"But they could be anywhere," Bess pointed out.

"Maybe," I said. My mind was working furiously.

"Or maybe not." They'd have to store them where no one else would find them by accident. And where the smell wouldn't seem out of place . . .

Grabbing my bag and my jacket, I headed for the door. "In fact," I said, "I think I have a very good idea where to look!"

12

Hooking the Crooks

W ait! Where are you going?" Bess demanded.

"Back to the marina," I said. "I have an idea where the barrels might be hidden."

"But, Nan!" Bess protested. "It's almost ten at night!"

"That's an advantage, actually," I said. "The marina is closed, so there won't be anybody there. And I can't afford to wait. Snead and Solomon must be planning to get rid of that waste permanently—if they haven't already done it. I've got to find it before that happens."

"Well, I'm going with you," Bess declared. "You can't go by yourself." She started to swing her legs off the bed, then groaned in agony. "Ow, ow!"

"Bess," I said. "You can't go with me. You can't even walk."

"I'll manage," Bess insisted. Pulling herself to her feet, she hobbled to her closet. "Just let me get my shoes. Ouch! Oooooh!"

"Seriously, Bess. There's no point in you coming with me. If we did happen to bump into Snead or Solomon, you wouldn't even be able to run away," I told her. "Please. Stay here. I really appreciate you wanting to help, but to be honest, you'd only slow me down."

"Well, call Ned, then," Bess said. "Or George."

"Ned's in the library, and that means his phone is turned off," I said. "And didn't George go to a basketball game tonight? Look, stop worrying. I'm just going to have a look around, that's all. I'll be fine."

"All right," Bess finally said, scowling. "But you have to promise to stay in touch with me, Nancy. Call me every five minutes, okay?"

"That's too much," I said, laughing. "I'll call you every half hour, how about that? If you don't hear from me, you can bring in the cavalry."

"Every fifteen minutes!" Bess called after me as I hurried down the stairs. "If I don't hear from you, I'm calling the mayor!"

Still chuckling, I jumped in my car and drove to the marina. I parked my car as inconspicuously as I could, in a spot that was partially screened by some bushes. Then I opened the trunk and took out what

George calls my "special detective bag." It's just a small black leather backpack in which I keep a few useful tools. I slung it over one shoulder.

Other than my car, the parking lot was empty. A single bulb burned over the door to the marina office. I could hear the faint creaking of the mooring lines as the boats rocked in the gentle river current. Otherwise, it was dark and quiet.

I sniffed the cool night air. Again I caught that faint whiff of burned cabbage and stinky socks. My heart beat faster. The waste barrels must still be here.

I walked quietly along the wooden walkway to the farthest dock. The old fishing trawler lay in its berth. I moved around the outside to be sure it was unoccupied. Then I set my foot on the deck and swung myself over the rail.

Brrrzzz! Brrrrzzz! I leaped about a foot in the air before I realized that the high-pitched ring-tone that suddenly shattered the quiet was coming from my pocket. I fished out my phone and squinted at the caller ID, my heart still racing. It was Bess.

I flipped open the phone before it could ring again. "Hello?" I whispered.

"It's been twenty minutes. You didn't call!" Bess said accusingly.

"Sorry!" I said, still whispering. "Look, I'm fine,

but I can't talk right now. I'll call you as soon as I can, all right?"

I hung up before she could reply. I set my phone on Vibrate, then returned it to my pocket.

The trawler was a big, heavy boat with a square cabin that rose up in the middle of the deck. The hatch was locked with a padlock, which I'd been expecting. I happen to own a lock-picking kit (for which Chief McGinnis would probably throw me in jail if he ever found out), and it's come in handy more times than I can count. Tonight I thanked my lucky stars for it one more time. Selecting a slender skewer-like tool, I inserted it into the lock mechanism and jiggled it gently. After a moment or two, there was a faint click as the padlock snapped open. I grinned to myself. "Yes!"

I unthreaded the padlock and pushed the door open. The cabin inside was almost completely dark—although my eyes had adjusted pretty well to the night outside, in here, all I could make out was some vague shapes. I put my lock-pick set back into my pack and pulled out a flashlight. Flicking it on, I aimed it around the inside of the trawler.

To my surprise, the cabin looked like an apartment. There was a little kitchenette—I suppose I should call it a galley—in one corner, and a table with seats around it. At the far end a short flight of stairs, called a *companionway* in boating lingo, led down to what I guessed was a bedroom. The whole place was clearly occupied. This must be where Bill Snead lived, I realized with a shock. Lucky for me he wasn't home! But I needed to work fast—he could come back at any moment.

I descended the companionway to the inner cabin. The smell of burned cabbage was stronger down here. Most of the small cabin was taken up by a sleeping bunk. There were no barrels, though, nor could I spot any place where they might be hidden.

Unless . . . I had an idea. Setting down my flashlight on a metal locker, I grasped the thin mattress in both hands and lifted up a corner. My eyes widened.

The platform under the mattress was a storage locker. It had a big hatch set into its top. I grasped the ring handle and, with an effort, heaved it up a few inches.

I couldn't see anything—the darkness under there was total. But the smell was stronger than ever, practically choking me. "Ugh," I gasped.

I lowered the hatch cover and grabbed the flashlight. Holding it between my teeth, I again lifted up the cover as far as I could.

Jackpot. Lying on their sides in the large locker under the bed were two rusting metal barrels. Flaking red paint on the side of each read SOLOMON PAPER.

I'd found the missing toxic waste!

Light suddenly flooded the cabin. "Well, well," a gravelly voice drawled behind me. "Looks to me like we've got a problem here."

I dropped the hatch cover and spun around, my heart pounding.

There, leaning in the doorway, looking down at me, was Bill Snead!

13

Trapped in a Net

Reacting on pure instinct, I hurled myself forward and drove my shoulder into Snead's knees. With a cry, he toppled over backward.

I scrambled up the companionway. But as I tried to step around him, Snead's hand shot out and grabbed my ankle. "Oh no, you don't," he grunted.

I kicked and struggled, but he hung on. "Help!" I yelled as loudly as I could. I doubted there was anyone nearby enough to hear me, but you never know.

Then, miracle of miracles, I heard footsteps on the deck outside! There was someone out there!

"Help!" I yelled again.

A figure filled the doorway. When I saw who it was, my heart sank all the way into my toes.

Richard Solomon.

Still, I had to at least try to fake my way out of this.

"Mr. Solomon!" I exclaimed. "Thank goodness you're here. I shouldn't have come inside, I know, but the cabin was unlocked and this afternoon I dropped the ring Ned gave me and I was hoping I could find keys to the office in here—"

I broke off as Solomon waved his hand. "Save it, Nancy," he said in a somber voice. "I've been asking around about you. I know enough about you to be certain that you're not here by accident. No, I'm afraid you've been snooping."

I sagged in Snead's grasp. Well, it had been worth a try.

"Hand me a length of rope from the locker on deck there, Rick," Snead said. "I'm going to tie her up."

Solomon stepped away from the hatchway and I heard him rummaging on deck. A moment later he reappeared with a coiled length of rope in his hand. He handed it to Snead, who set about tying me up. Any hope I had that he might do a sloppy job vanished as I saw how efficiently he handled the rope. Obviously, this was a man who knew how to tie knots.

In a matter of minutes, my wrists were bound and my feet were lashed together. Snead pushed me down onto one of the bench seats that surrounded the table, then tied the rope around my wrists to the post at the end of the bench.

"I found her in the inner cabin," he told Solomon as he worked. "She had the locker open. She saw everything."

"That's too bad," Solomon said, shaking his head. "I'm very sorry to hear that."

The crazy thing was, he really did sound sorry. I guess that's what made me blurt out the thing that had been in my mind ever since I realized he was behind the whole mystery. "How could you do it, Mr. Solomon?" I asked. "You've made the environment the centerpiece of your campaign for governor. People really believed you meant it when you said you'd protect our woods and waterways. How could you of all people be responsible for poisoning the land with toxic waste?"

"Never you mind," Snead growled, but Solomon held up a hand.

"No, it's all right," he said. "I'd like to answer that."

Snead snorted but said nothing.

Stepping into the cabin, Richard Solomon took a seat opposite me. He swept his salt-and-pepper hair back from his forehead and then clasped his hands in front of him on the table. He looked as if he were giving an interview.

"You have to understand," he said, giving me an earnest look, "that this was more than twenty years ago. We were just kids, Bill and me, and we didn't know then what we know about toxic waste now."

Hah! I thought. Twenty years ago, people had known plenty about the damage to the environment caused by toxic waste dumping. I remembered learning in elementary school about the environmental disaster called Love Canal—that had happened almost thirty years ago. Ignorance was a flimsy excuse. But I didn't say anything. I didn't want to make Solomon angry. Not when I was tied up and helpless.

"The Environmental Protection Agency was on its way to inspect my father's plant. We'd managed to dispose of most of our waste within the new EPA guidelines, but we had these two barrels that were still unprocessed. The problem was, we were over our limit, and the plant had already been fined the previous year for violations," Solomon went on. "We knew that if the inspectors found violations again, the consequences would be severe. They might even shut down the plant. That would have been a tragedy for River Heights—Solomon Paper has been a top local employer for almost fifty years."

"Not as big a tragedy as polluting our river," I couldn't help pointing out.

Solomon frowned. "That's a matter of opinion, I think. But, anyway.

"These two barrels—two little barrels of sludge—could spell the end of Solomon Paper. I couldn't stand by and let that happen, so I asked Bill to help me take care of them. We brought them over to a piece of undeveloped land on the far side of what was then a scrap metal yard. We figured it was land that no one would ever think of developing, and so the barrels would be out of harm's way there."

And also, your father's plant would be saved so that you could inherit it, I thought. But this time, I managed to keep quiet.

"And that's where they stayed, until the Half Moon Bay condos came along," Solomon went on. "When it became clear that construction was going to start soon, I realized we had to do something. We couldn't leave those barrels there if people were going to be living on that land." He gave me a crooked smile. "I know this may sound strange coming from me, but I couldn't be that irresponsible."

At this, Snead, who was standing behind Richard Solomon, rolled his eyes.

"You're right," I said. "It does sound strange. Are you sure you weren't just moving them because you were afraid they'd be found and people would trace them back to you?"

Solomon bit his lip and looked down. "Ouch," he said. "I suppose I deserve that. And yes, I have to admit that you're right. I *was* afraid of being found out. But not just because I didn't want to get into trouble. It's also because I really believe I could do some good as governor of this state, and it just seemed, well, wrong to let this one thing from the past—the distant past— jeopardize the future. Not when Bill and I could so easily just remove the barrels." He leaned back in his seat. "In the years since then, you see, waste disposal has come a long way, and there's no question we can dispose of this small amount of sludge without any measurable environmental impact."

"I still say it'd be easier to just dump 'em in the river," Snead muttered.

Solomon's face darkened, but he made no response.

"But it's already had an impact!" I argued. "What about the toxins found in the river fish? One of your barrels leaked, Mr. Solomon!"

"That's unproven," Solomon replied easily. "Those toxins could have come from another source. But let's suppose you're right, and the barrel did leak. The reality is, toxins in moving water wash away quickly. Once the source of pollution is removed, which it has been, in a few months the river will be as clean as it ever was." He smiled and held up his hands. "No harm done!"

I felt a chill that had nothing to do with the

temperature in the boat cabin. Richard Solomon is completely crazy, I realized. Or, at the very least, he was such a good salesman that he was able to convince himself that what he was saying was actually reasonable. It was, in a way, the scariest moment I'd had since I'd started investigating this case.

The next moment, though, it got even scarier.

"The question now is, what are we going to do with you?" Solomon said.

"Well," I said hopefully, "you could just let me go. That would be the right thing to do."

He laughed politely, as if I'd just made a not-very-funny joke. "It depends on how you look at it."

"Rick, we're wasting time." Snead, who'd been listening silently all this time, now spoke up with impatience in his voice. "I know what to do with her. We take her downriver a few miles, pick a good deep spot, rope her up to one of these barrels here, and drop 'em both overboard."

I bit back a gasp of terror.

"We can't do that, Bill," Solomon said in a patient voice. "We've been over this before."

Huh? I stared at Solomon. Was he going to let me go after all?

"The barrels are not going in the river," Solomon went on. "If we do that, it's only a matter of time before they rust through and all the sludge spills out.

That would be an environmental catastrophe. No. The barrels are going to the waste facility."

"I still think that's asking for trouble," Snead grumbled.

"No one is paying you to think," Solomon snapped. "That's my job, remember?"

There was a long silence while the two men glared at each other. I held my breath. Clearly there was a lot of tension between Snead and Solomon. If only Snead would throw a punch!

In the midst of the silence, my back pocket suddenly started to hum as if there were a dozen bees in it. My cell phone! It had to be Bess, calling to check up on me. When I didn't answer, she'd realize something was wrong and call for help. Wouldn't she? She had to!

The phone let out a hum as it vibrated again. Uh-oh! I thought. What if Snead or Solomon hears that? If they think someone might come looking for me, I'm dead right now!

I had to cover up the noise. Taking a deep breath, I put my head down and started to fake-sob. "Please don't hurt me," I wailed. "Please, please, let me go. I promise I won't tell anyone about this. I just want to go home. Please!"

"Nancy," Solomon said in a gentle voice. "Nancy. You know we can't let you go. I'm so sorry, but that's the way it has to be. You do understand why, don't you?"

The phone seemed to have stopped vibrating. I lifted my head, still sniffling. "Please?" I said again, faintly.

Solomon just gave me a sad smile.

Snead was still scowling, but he seemed to have gotten hold of his temper. "All right, then, what do you want to do with the girl?" he asked in a surly tone.

"We can follow your plan. It's crude, but effective—only we'll weight Nancy's legs with one of your mooring blocks instead of a barrel," Solomon said calmly. "At least that will be environmentally neutral."

Talk about cold-blooded!

"Whatever," Solomon muttered. "I'll get the engine fired up, then."

He stomped out of the cabin. A moment later I heard the deep, coughing roar of the trawler's powerful engine as it sputtered to life.

Solomon rose from his seat. "I'd better give Bill a hand," he murmured, and stepped outside as well.

His utter creepiness made me feel cold all over, but I knew I had no time to think about that right now. If I had any hope of escaping, I had to try to free my hands while I was alone.

Scooting to the edge of the seat, I bent forward

and began trying to pick the knot apart with my teeth. The rope Snead had used was tough and filled with sharp fibers that poked my lips. "Ow, ow!" I said under my breath as I chewed away.

The throb of the boat's engine rose to a higher pitch. Then the boat jerked gently into motion. My heart jerked along with it. I was running out of time!

The more I gnawed at the rope, though, the more I realized that it was hopeless. It was far too thick and tough for me to chew through, and the knot must have been one of those complicated ones that sailors use. I couldn't figure out where it began and ended, let alone how to untie it.

If I hadn't been panicking before, I definitely was now. This was one of the tightest spots I'd ever been in. Every moment was bringing me closer to the stretch of water where Snead and Solomon planned to dump me. And now that we were on the river, how would Bess ever find me?

I swallowed hard. Was this the end?

"No!" I said out loud. I would not give up! Leaning forward, I began to nibble at the rope once more.

The vibration at my hip startled me again, making me jerk forward and whack my cheek against the knotted rope. "Bess, where are you?" I muttered. "I really need you to bring in the cavalry now!"

It seemed like only a few minutes later that the

sound of the trawler's engine dropped to a lower pitch. I shuddered as Snead and then Solomon stepped through the hatchway.

"I'm afraid it's time," Solomon told me. "Once again, Nancy, I want to tell you how sorry I am. You don't know how I wish there was another way."

"Oh, I think I have some idea," I managed.

As Snead untied me from the beam, I did my best to struggle and slow him down. But he simply picked me up and heaved me over his shoulder like a sack of potatoes. He stepped through the hatch again with me on his shoulder.

"You won't get away with this!" I yelled. "My friends all know I'm here! When I don't come back, they'll know you had something to do with it!"

"You're probably lying. Of course, you might not be, but that's a chance we'll have to take, I guess," Solomon said calmly.

Snead set me down on the deck. Then Solomon held me still while Snead wrapped the chain from the mooring block around my ankles. He snapped the shackle closed, then gave it a tug to test it. "All set," he announced.

I felt like I was about to faint. Maybe that's why I didn't quite take it in when the night was suddenly lit up by the beam of a powerful spotlight.

But when I heard Chief McGinnis's voice blaring, "Stop what you're doing!" I began to realize that Bess—and the cavalry—had arrived in the nick of time.

14

Reeling in a Big One

What happened after that is kind of a blur in my mind. I remember Solomon and Snead cursing and yelling at each other. Each one seemed to think it was the other one's fault that they'd been caught.

Then uniformed water patrol officers were climbing over the rails of the trawler, followed by Bess, George, and Ned. The three of them ran to me where I lay on the deck. "I told you it was dangerous!" Bess kept saying. "I told you!" Normally I hate it when people say "I told you so," but she was laughing and sobbing at the same time, and somehow I couldn't get annoyed.

Ned held me in his arms while Bess and George untangled the chain around my feet. Then one of the water unit officers pulled out a knife and sliced through the ropes that bound my hands and feet. I didn't feel strong enough to stand up yet, so I just sat on the deck. "Thanks for rescuing me," I told my friends with a weak smile. "For a while there, I really thought I was done for."

"Not with Bess around," George said. "After the first time you didn't answer your phone, she didn't waste any time calling out the troops."

"She drove to my house and made me wake up my dad," Ned chimed in. "She knew we'd need police help, and she figured if the publisher of the local newspaper called Chief McGinnis, he'd have to take us seriously."

"And then when we drove to the marina and you weren't here but the trawler was moving downriver, Bess is the one who convinced the chief that you were on it," George finished.

"You're a superhero," I told Bess. I reached out to hug her, but since I was still sitting down, the only part of her I could reach was her knees. I put my arms around them.

"Ow!" she exclaimed.

By this time, Chief McGinnis had managed to climb awkwardly onboard the trawler. When he saw Richard Solomon, his face went a little pale—he didn't often have to arrest such important people—but nevertheless, he stepped forward. "Richard Solomon and William Snead, you are under arrest for kidnapping," he said in a formal voice. "You have the right to remain silent. Anything you say can and may be used against you in a court of law. You have the right to an attorney. . . ."

As the chief finished telling them their rights, I struggled to my feet. "I think you'll want to add to those charges when I show you what I found inside," I told him. "And when I tell you about the last couple of days. For example, Bill Snead is the one who broke into the Nickersons' house and attacked Ned's mother."

Snead scowled. "I told you that was a stupid idea," he spat at Solomon. "This whole thing is your fault, beginning to end. I told you we should have—"

"Shut up, you idiot!" Solomon snapped. "Don't you even have the brains to keep your mouth shut?"

"I'll show you brains!" Snead bellowed. He would have lunged at Solomon right there on deck if the police officers hadn't held him back.

"Get 'em into the patrol boat," Chief McGinnis ordered the officers. Then he turned to me. "So," he said in a fake-casual tone. "I guess you're going to give James Nickerson a big story for the *Bugle*, huh?"

I grinned. Chief McGinnis is a great chief of police, but he hates it when anyone else gets credit for solving crimes in River Heights.

"I wouldn't do that," I assured him. "I need to keep a low profile—I can't solve mysteries if all the crooks know who I am. Anyway, you're the one who caught the bad guys in a spectacular nighttime chase on the river."

"I guess I am, at that," he agreed, his face brightening.

"This is your story, Chief," I said. "I'm just glad my friends and I were here to see how it all went down."

You could practically see the chief's chest swelling. "Just doing my job, protecting the citizens of our fair town," he said. "Now, why don't you refresh my memory on the details, Nancy. . . ."

About a week later, Ned, Bess, George, and I met up at Mugged. Bess came in after the rest of us, her nose buried in the latest edition of the *River Heights Bugle*.

"It's kind of sad," she said as she took her seat. "Richard Solomon seemed like such a great guy. I think a lot of people would have voted for him for governor."

"I definitely would have," George said.

"Yeah, me too," Ned agreed. He looked dejected. "I had no idea he was such a crook."

"No one did," I said, laying my hand gently on his arm. "And, to be fair to Richard Solomon, I do believe there was a lot of good in him. I think he was perfectly sincere about all the reforms and changes he wanted to make as governor."

"Unfortunately, he just happened to be a psycho at the same time," George added.

"Well," I said, trying to change the subject to something less painful for Ned, "at least your dad's paper is doing well with the story, Ned."

"They sure are," he said. "Articles from the *Bugle* have been picked up by major papers from New York to San Francisco. This story is really big!"

"And Chief McGinnis is claiming all the credit for catching Snead and Solomon," Bess said with a sniff. "Honestly, Nancy, doesn't it drive you crazy sometimes the way he hogs the spotlight?"

I laughed. "A little," I admitted. "But I meant what I said to him on the boat that night. I really do prefer to stay in the background. It's better for me if the crooks around here think I'm just an average teenage girl."

"Instead of a beautiful young supersleuth," Ned said, taking my hand in his and giving it a squeeze.

I blushed. Ned can always make me blush.

George stood up from the table, brushing muffin crumbs off her sweats. "Well, guys," she said, "I'd better get going. Nancy, Ned, are we meeting at six tomorrow morning?"

Ned and I groaned together. "Yes, master," I droned. "Your slaves will be there, ready to run as you crack the whip."

"Ahhh," Bess said, her eyes twinkling mischievously. "While I will still be lying in bed, dreaming of not running." After two days of excruciating leg cramps, Bess had backed out of training for the charity run. "I don't care if Deirdre wins," she'd said. "I will never run again, if I can possibly avoid it. It's clearly hazardous to my health!"

Luckily, I'd been able to recruit Ned to our team, so George and I were still training. Honestly, though I'd never tell Bess this, having Ned on the team meant that we at least had a chance of winning. He was a much better runner. Of course, now that Richard Solomon was in jail and awaiting his criminal trial, he probably wouldn't be matching the winner's pledge earnings, but the race was still for a great cause.

We were all saying good-bye when Ned's cell phone rang. "Hi, Dad," he said after he answered it. "What's that? . . . Oh, no. You've got to be kidding!"

Bess, George, and I gave one another questioning looks.

"Do me a favor, will you," Ned said into the phone. "Can you e-mail it to me right now? I want Nancy to have a look at it."

Hanging up, he sat down again and pulled out

his laptop. (The police had found it, and his camera, when they'd searched Richard Solomon's home after his arrest. The pictures had all been deleted, but Ned's computer still had his Victorian poetry paper on it, which was a piece of luck!)

Ned booted up and used his wireless connection to open his e-mail account. "Check this out," he said to me as he clicked on the e-mail that had just arrived from his dad.

Bess, George, and I crowded together to peer over his shoulder. My mouth fell open as a photo filled the screen. It was Ned's shot of his father and the catfish!

"I totally forgot that I'd e-mailed these shots to Dad," Ned explained. "He had them on his work computer the whole time!"

"You mean, even though Richard Solomon went to all that trouble to steal all the copies of the incriminating pictures, the publisher of the *Bugle* had these in his possession all the while?" George asked. "You have to admit that's kind of funny."

"It is, I agreed. "And here's what's even funnier. Look!" I pointed at the screen. Behind Mr. Nickerson, the shoreline was barely visible in the rising sun. Where Snead and Solomon had dug up the toxic waste, all you could make out was a black, blurry silhouette. It wasn't even possible to tell that it was a human shape.

"Oh, I don't believe it," Bess muttered. "They went to all that trouble for a picture of . . ."

"Of nothing in particular," I finished for her. "In fact, if they *hadn't* bothered to try to hide the evidence of their crime, it's more than likely that no one would ever have found out about it. How's that for funny?"

For a second longer, Ned sat there looking glum. Then, slowly, a smile spread across his face. He began to chuckle. "I guess when you look at it that way, it is kind of ridiculous," he admitted.

"Totally," Bess agreed, giggling.

"Completely," George added.

"Utterly!" I chimed in, and we all sat there in the coffee shop, laughing like a bunch of idiots.